T0120507

AN OFF THE MAT MYSTERY

# TARA SHELDON

FOR THOSE WHO BEND

*and*

FOR THOSE WHO DO NOT

*and of course,*

FOR EMMA AND GRAHAM

**IT WAS SAID,** sometimes to her face but more often behind her back, that she did not look like a yoga instructor. As if that weren't enough, her name, cast as it was in some vague Euro mold, came suspiciously close to sounding grandiose.

On the occasion remarks about her looks reached her, Eugenie would say, "That's marketing for you," which meant she never expected to be included in the photos of teachers posted on the website. If quizzed on her name, she would reply, smile retreating, that her mother had been a fan of Napoleon.

On this still dark May morning, Eugenie entered a security code in the keypad which, after a predictable but nonetheless always worrisome pause, clicked open the front door to the yoga studio. She promptly fell over Nandy, the owner's dog. Eugenie's weight didn't do the terrier any favors and Nandy yelped in pain.

"Nandy Shakyamuni Shantideva Wetherell!" cried a voice from the back. "Could you make any more racket?"

To Eugenie's disappointment, it was the studio owner who, despite the time, looked as ever as though menopause had passed her by.

"Oh, it's only you," the owner said. "I knew someone had scheduled an early class."

Scooping up the dog with a startling grace, Martha Wetherell planted eyes on Eugenie. "Have you started your social media campaign? The one I told you about. It will bring in more students. All the other teachers have seen results."

Eugenie sighed, wondering if that was the case. As far as she knew, the studio's classes were mostly full and had been for months. Where would they put more students if they showed up?

"Chairs, we might need more," Eugenie replied, her voice still small from sleep.

"Naturally," said Martha. "For on-the-ass yoga as taught by Sarah."

"Eugenie," said Eugenie. "My name's…"

"Don't even try. I'll never remember," said Martha. "You and Sarah. I always get you two mixed up."

Eugenie felt her brow crease. Sarah was years younger and pounds lighter. It simply wasn't possible to confuse Eugenie with Sarah. Eugenie wondered if there was a full moon.

"Chair yoga will be given the respect it deserves, and soon. You watch! It's even been foretold the next Buddha will be sitting on a chair," said Martha, pointing a defiant finger skyward as she lowered the dog, who promptly returned to its place blocking the front door.

The sun wasn't yet up, and Martha was ready to take on the world. For the thousandth time, Eugenie wondered about her own lack of ambition and drive. She was miles away from Martha in temperament, not to mention body mass index. If Martha was a type A, Eugenie was a type Z.

And yet, Eugenie's students were deeply loyal. She watched as they filed in, carefully stepping over the dog, then making their way to one of three classrooms.

"This time work for everyone?" Eugenie asked when they had gathered. The students nodded and one, Jared, spoke up. "A reason not to punch the alarm for the fifth time." The group murmured in agreement.

"Great, we'll start," said Eugenie. "First, let's set an intention, either for ourselves or for someone we love."

Eugenie paused, allowing the class to settle. When there was no more shifting in chairs, she let herself go inward. The usual intention that she guide the class in a way that was supportive of each student did not seem right. Something was off; she could feel it.

Scanning her body, she found her ankle throbbed from the encounter with Nandy, and her stomach, despite a hastily downed clump of granola, growled. She forced her attention to the surrounding space. The light from the overhead spot, even though set on the usual low, beamed too bright. The music from her playlist sounded unfamiliar, a ridiculous thought, as she was the one who picked it.

"Breathe," she reminded herself.

On his chair, Jared shifted. Not, Eugenie knew at once, because he was uncomfortable but because he was trying to attract her attention to get this thing started. The move was so obvious, and Jared was so used to having his way, Eugenie responded by cueing in a voice that sounded, even to her, a little unfamiliar.

"Let's get the circulation going by raising arms in parallel to the sky," said Eugenie. "Then down to prayer position, hands pressed together in front of heart center. Repeat at your own pace five times."

Eugenie looked out at the class, relieved to see that for once the students had arranged their chairs with plenty of space in between, reducing the possibility of a collision when the postures began. Having come to several of her classes, they knew by now what to expect.

The thought reassured her, and she continued in a more confident voice: "Inhale on the upward movement and exhale on the downward. If you feel pain during the class, back off to a place of no pain. Your body is wise. Let it guide you."

Looking down at her soft belly, Eugenie wondered, was *her* body wise? Hadn't it for years told her to pass up the chips and cookies? And hadn't each time, probably millions by now, her mouth overruled her brain?

As she pondered the question, moments passed, and the class entered the hand and wrist sequence. Eugenie always struggled through this section, although her students made it plain they benefited. Several worked long hours at keyboards and were prone to carpal tunnel issues.

Even though she knew that, she felt herself speed up, as if wanting to get the movements done. Not good, she thought. She had fallen into the mental trap of checking off boxes, a warning sign for any teacher. Slow down, she told herself, come back to the moment.

"Bring each finger to the center of the palm," she cued. "First thumb, then pointer, then middle, then ring, then little and now back to ring."

Her ring finger hadn't had a ring on it for, what was it now, ten years? Her husband had gone off with, of all things, a yoga instructor. The irony was not lost on Eugenie, and she felt her teeth clench.

Someone cleared their throat. The sound brought Eugenie back from her thoughts and she addressed the class: "Now bring attention to your wrists by clasping fingers together and tracing the infinity symbol, a sideways figure eight. Choose the direction which draws you and then, for balance sake, we'll repeat in reverse."

Eugenie started to the left probably, she realized, because as a child she was left-handed. Her mother, governed in most ways by superstition, believed Eugenie's preference ominous, and demanded her daughter switch. Early on, the message that things were not right came through loud and clear.

From the front row, one student, Eugenie knew her name as Callie, winced in pain.

"You okay?" asked Eugenie.

"My arthritis, no surprise," responded Callie. "Worse some days than others."

"Gently shake your hands out," said Eugenie. "And perhaps a small massage, like this," continued Eugenie, demonstrating.

"Helps, thanks," replied Callie.

"Good," said Eugenie. "Remember everyone, this class, like every class, is your gift to yourself. We're all trying to find that perfect spot, the 'edge' some call it. That place of stretch that challenges us but doesn't bring pain and stop the breath," Eugenie said, then paused. "Not too much to ask."

The class laughed and Jared shot out, "Not too much to ask if you know where the hell that place is."

Eugenie had pegged Jared as the youngest in class and the little she knew about him she wished she didn't. He had been a pro football player with a brilliant career. Then, in an opening game against a know-nothing opponent, he'd been injured. TV cameras captured the hit and ran it over and over so that millions, even those who would have preferred not to, saw it. And no one who saw failed to gasp; it was that bad. Hospitalized, then put on medication, Jared's recovery was slow. Out of frustration, one of his doctors recommended yoga.

In the background, Eugenie could hear music play from the room's speakers. She listened closely to see if she was behind or ahead of where she should be in the sequence of postures. A violin concerto began, and she relaxed, relieved that for the moment, she was on the mark.

For the play list, she had chosen a collection of pan flute, spa, classical, harmonium, and waterfall sounds. Like disc jockeys, yoga teachers were proud of their playlists, and it had taken many tries to get the mix right. To start, she had chosen a pipe melody to help cue breathing. As she had often observed, most people were chest breathers, inhaling tight gasps which never reached the belly. Less likely with this piece of music, she was convinced. If nothing else, it would help students loosen up their diaphragms, allowing breath to flow easily and deeply, as mother nature intended.

And yet, her diaphragm was not loose. What is wrong? she wondered again. Could it be the fact class was now earlier? A screech from the window behind her interrupted the thought. It sounded like an old bicycle rattling, broken chain and all.

And in Eugenie's state of mind, that noise summed up everything that was off that morning.

And yet, she reminded herself, yogis were taught to believe nothing was ever "wrong." That whatever was happening was happening for a purpose and was exactly as it should be. This view, Eugenie was first to admit, she hadn't mastered and as if to prove the point, she reached down to console her throbbing ankle. One student, thinking this was a cue to a posture, responded by doing the same.

Embarrassed, Eugenie shook her head and slowly, she began a torso movement, hands on thighs and core moving in every direction. Her students got the message and followed, each deep in the gentle movement of the sequence. She heard their breathing go soft and rhythmic. Next to a student snoring during the resting pose at the end of class, that sound was the most flattering a teacher could hear.

She tried to feel gratitude, but her monkey mind would not let her. The mental chatter she was so proud of keeping at bay was in that moment, overwhelming. She could feel her forehead tense as she responded to what was now a barrage of memories, opinions, questions, to-do lists, and irritations. For the umpteenth time, she reminded herself she was a yoga teacher.

She had studied. She had practiced. She had good intentions. She cared about her students. She had put in her time.

She, Eugenie, did not deserve this, whatever this was.

From the speaker, the play list continued with waterfall sounds signaling the time for relaxation. Eugenie found her voice and managed to get out the words, "Attend to your breath, for in breath, there is peace. Just breathe. Breathe." A slight shifting in chairs, and the room fell silent.

It was there in this quietest of spaces that a fire alarm rang out. Eugenie watched as her students' eyes grew wide. Someone in the back jumped up, knocking over a chair.

"Thank you, Jesus," said Jared, throwing up his hands as he kicked the chair out of the way. "I was about to piss my pants from all that water."

## "ANYONE SEEN THE dog?"

Her ears still ringing from the alarm, Eugenie was barely able to make out Martha's question and then the "Nandy! Nandy! Nandy!" that followed.

Eugenie looked around. She had not known this place outside the back door of the studio even existed. Hands on hips, she surveyed the view. Mist rising from a pond surrounded on one side by a thatch of reeds, spindly pine trees, and determined palms had turned everything the palest lavender. The morning was still cool, and in her tights, she shivered slightly.

"What happened?" Callie asked. "Is there a fire?"

"I didn't smell smoke," someone noted.

"The dog!" Martha repeated. "Where's Nandy? If anything has happened to that dog, I'll never..."

From out of the dense brush appeared a firefighter. "You looking for this pipsqueak?" he asked. The firefighter was as big as some of the smaller palm trees, and in his arms, the terrier looked the size of a coconut.

"Nandy," Martha sighed, taking the dog from him.

"Out of my way, folks!" ordered the firefighter, and the spandex-swaddled group stepped aside. A group, Eugenie noticed, that no longer included Jared.

"I still don't smell any smoke," one of Eugenie's students said.

"Martha, do you?" asked Eugenie.

"Nothing," said Martha, holding Nandy close. "I don't smell a thing but from what I was told when we installed the alarm system, smoke or no smoke, fire or no fire, the crew now has to examine the whole studio which may take, I don't know, a while, let's say. Best go on with your day."

Taking in the thick vegetation around them, one student asked, "So if we can't go back inside, what're we supposed to do?"

"The path between the pickerelweed will bring you to the parking lot," Martha said, pointing. "There, you can't miss it."

"But our shoes!" one student exclaimed, looking at her bare feet.

"More to the point, our car keys!" said another. "Both still in the studio."

"I guess you'll have to wait," said Martha. "All of us will have to wait until we get the okay."

By now the sun had cleared the line of reeds and palms, rising above even the tallest of the scrub pines, and it was getting hot. Eugenie wiped the sweat from her eyes and addressed the group, "Enough already. Who's up for finding some shade?"

"I'm staying put," said Martha. "In case they have questions, I want the crew to know where to find me."

"Everyone else?" Eugenie asked, and the group nodded.

It took some time, but Eugenie found what only in the most generous sense could be called the path between the pickerelweed and she started toward it, walking on tiptoe. From over her shoulder, Martha's voice railed: "Not like that! Noise! Make lots of noise, so whatever's out there knows you're coming."

As if on cue, a lizard dashed in front of Eugenie's foot, missing by a snout getting squashed. "Ugh," thought Eugenie, but it was "Om," that came out of her mouth. Instead of laughing, the group took up the mantra, and in the next instant, there came from the assembled a vibration strong enough to startle a bear.

Despite the chorus, Eugenie wasn't completely convinced, and she continued to keep an eye out for snakes on the ground and spiders in the air. Thinking they might encounter webs strung between the crowded limbs, she considered grabbing a branch, then concluded the firefighter's presence on the path must have cleared them and maybe also scared off any snakes.

Then again, maybe not. There were some nasty spiders out there and try as she might, she struggled to feel compassion. This led her to pick up a loose branch. Using it, she swept the air. Her footsteps, also not completely reassured, now landed hard on the ground, announcing, to any creature with ears or sense, every inch of her progress.

Then finally, to her relief, the group was safely back at the front of the building. As Eugenie dislodged a twig from between her toes, Jared appeared at her side.

"Where'd you go?" she asked, not looking up.

"In the john. Firefighter tore me a new one when he saw I hadn't evacuated," said Jared with a laugh. "After the sermon, he said, 'Wait, don't I know you? From TV?' He'd seen the hit. Can you believe it? 'Aren't you supposed to be dead?' the guy asked." Jared threw his head back and roared, "Dead, so that's it. I'm supposed to be dead!"

Eugenie wasn't laughing. "You ignore the obvious and one day you might be."

"Aww, lighten up," said Jared. "There was no fire, no emergency, no nothing. The alarm just went off."

"In my experience," Eugenie said, "Alarms do not just go off."

"Well, in mine, they do," said Jared. "Alarms go off, timers go off, bombs go off, even people... go off."

Then, as if to emphasize his smarts, Jared flung keys in the air, deftly catching them behind his back. Confident that Eugenie still watched, he sauntered to his car, flip flops clicking loudly to underscore each departing step.

*3*

**LEFT TO HER** own ways, Eugenie would never have splurged on a yearly pass to the beach at the end of the causeway.

It was Lizbeth who made it possible: Lizbeth, who was so worn out by being on her feet most days, she thrilled at the idea of doing yoga while sitting on a chair; Lizbeth, who worked for some federal agency and did something she couldn't talk about, who was then transferred somewhere she couldn't say.

"In appreciation of all things learned," said her card to Eugenie and tucked into the envelope was the gift of a year's admission to this lovely beach.

Eugenie showed the pass to the ranger and drove in through the gate. Reading the welcome sign, Eugenie thought, was it true that the sand here was the whitest in the country, the shells more abundant, or was that the usual advertising hype?

As she advanced on the narrow road, the next sign tore through the illusion: "Stay on the paths! Rattlesnakes in the area."

Rattlesnakes were in the area alright. Eugenie had seen one the other day. Making her way to the far end of the beach, she parked her car, the only one in the lot.

Moments later she was chin deep in the surf, the events of the morning beginning to fade. The saltwater cure, her father called it. There was nothing, no anxiety, sadness, confusion, no grief, no betrayal, nothing that saltwater couldn't cure, or so he said.

That he never went near a beach was not to be mentioned.

A few feet into the water, Eugenie felt the sand under her toes give way and she began a tentative breaststroke. Against her hands, the water parted. Warm as piss in August, or so the local expression went, the temperature in May still had the power to shock. Her breath quickened.

There could be danger in the most unexpected places. Even poor, gentle Lizbeth had been touched by it. Shortly after her transfer, she died. The word was violently. The yoga practice Eugenie loved brought to her all kinds of people: those, like Lizbeth who suffered through tough jobs but also those who'd been in car accidents, some only recently cleared from surgery. A few, maybe more than a few, who'd been traumatized.

Jared.

He was angry, that much was clear. It came out in class. And once, when they were alone. But really, what did she know about him?

He'd been injured. He'd lost his career. He was in pain. In classes, he appeared to be trying.

Well, weren't we all, thought Eugenie.

Trying our damnedest to get through the day.

In the water, she felt something long and smooth brush against her. She gasped then yanked her leg away. A shark? She was no novice to the beach. She knew sharks combed these waters looking for food, especially near sandbars.

"Top of the food chain, don't you forget," she said aloud to the depths below. Then, "I am not brunch for you," she added, laughing. As if talking to a shark would have any effect. She tread water for a few minutes and felt only the resistance of the surf.

Reassured, she lay back, letting her long curly hair straighten in the waves. For a while, she bobbed up and down until the hastily applied sunscreen to her face felt like it was no longer doing its job. She paddled back to the beach, realizing that she did feel better. If only her father had known. It really was a miracle cure.

There was now a sprinkling of people on the shore. Above them, an osprey flew silent and low, its massive wingspan casting an undefined shadow on the sand. From somewhere down the beach came the sounds of rap music. "What'd you think it's there for, man? For you, man, for us, man. Your quest, man, go get it, no doubt, man, don't fret it, your fate, man, go get..."

Absently, she listened, face frowning. Then, turning her attention to her hair, she used a determined grasp to squeeze water from each section. Lifting her beach bag, she found her cell phone at the bottom. On it were three messages she quickly swiped through, simultaneously aware that Martha Wetherell would have read the entirety of each one and probably, Eugenie sighed, responded promptly in full and grammatically correct sentences. Eugenie threw the phone back in the bag and curled up against the curve of her beach umbrella and quickly fell asleep. Her mother, marveling at Eugenie's ability to fall asleep anywhere, anytime, would have remarked, "Lucky girl, she sleeps the sleep of the innocent."

But that, Eugenie knew, was no longer true.

While she slept on the beach, the familiar dream made itself known once again. The image of Jared looking much as he had that night: sheepish that he had looked up her address. ("Took me about two minutes on the net to find you.") And even more sheepish that he had such a lame excuse for visiting. "Martha said you had a book that might help." Then he couldn't remember the title, the author, or even what the book was about. At the door to her house, Eugenie had laughed.

In the dream, the laughter went on and on. Then, it cut to their clothes off, bodies pressed against the sheets of the bed she had not made that morning. "Get on top. Less pain that way," she heard him say, and she understood immediately he didn't mean her pain. Then there were no more words, only release. She and Jared had moved in sync the way only people with no expectation could do.

Afterward, he was grateful. So grateful she thought she might receive a thank you note and wondered if there was a Hallmark card for that.

But that was months ago.

"Lady, this yours? Lady!" an insistent male voice brought her back from sleep. "Wind carried it away."

Eugenie wiped her eyes and squinted. She thought she recognized the guy as one of the group who'd been playing rap. In his hands, he waved her umbrella back and forth.

"Another inch and it would have been on its way to China," he said. "Well, Texas, anyway."

"Yes," Eugenie responded, holding out her palm, "It's mine. Thanks. Thank you."

The young man nodded, turned, then paused, laughing. "That must have been some dream you were having. By the way you looked I mean. Just saying, it must have been some dream."

"Yes, well..." Eugenie replied, chucking her belongings back in the bag. As an afterthought, she shoved the umbrella, wet and sandy, against one startled armpit and headed for the car.

Not until she slammed the trunk did the laughter from the beach stop.

**4**

**THAT NIGHT IN** the studio bathroom, Eugenie wrestled with her tights. With each tug, she tried to convince herself the cause for them slipping was weight loss. But as she took in her curves in the mirror, she knew that was not the case. The tights had merely given up the battle against the fullness of her waist to rest on the relative slimness of her hips. Resigned, she reached behind her back to find the fabric of her top and realized that too was all wrong. The top should be longer. In the large studio with nine-feet-tall mirrors, the students couldn't fail to get a view of parts she wanted to keep to herself. She wondered again why in the world she had said yes to Sarah.

"Say you'll cover for me! Tonight. 7 pm.," Sarah had implored in her text message when Eugenie finally got around to reading it. And then, she added, "A mat, not a chair class."

"You would have to remind me of that, Sarah," groaned Eugenie to herself, "Because I'm the only one who teaches chair." Then Eugenie selected delete and moved on to the last message, which she would have erased without reading were it not for the number of exclamation points. Sarah must be getting frantic. "Eugenie! You teach all kinds of classes! You can do this! I know it's not what you usually teach, but it's not that different. I promise! Say you will. Oh, please!!!" The desperation was impossible to ignore, and Eugenie had headed home. After spending a half hour searching for notes to sequence a class acceptable to someone as picky as Sarah, Eugenie called her.

"Bullshit, you need notes," said Sarah when she found out.

"Well, it's just that it's not a class I usually cover," said Eugenie.

"Girl, would I ask if I didn't think you could do it? Besides," said Sarah. "Everyone else I asked said no."

"So, I'm your last resort," said Eugenie.

"Hey," said Sarah, "We were in teacher training together. You knew your stuff. Besides which, you're doing me a big favor. The gods are with you."

"From your lips," Eugenie sighed and hung up.

That night, after the struggle with her tights, Eugenie faced Sarah's class, which was bigger than any she'd taught in the past.

She straightened her spine and took in a deep breath. "Hi everyone. I'm Eugenie subbing for Sarah. If this is your first time, welcome. Anybody brand new?"

A few hands shot up and Eugenie asked if they had any health issues they wanted to share. "Slipped disc," one offered. Then another, "Old rotator cuff injury." Then a third, "Advanced age." The class chuckled. And finally, "Under 30 but no exercise since I was 14 when my mom insisted I had the makings of a prima ballerina."

"Okay, I can see everyone's in good spirits," Eugenie said. "Here's my best advice, for everybody no matter what age or condition, and especially for those new to the practice. Listen to yourself. You are your best guide. This is a place to honor your body. Pay attention to that and you will learn and grow, get strong, become more flexible, but not get injured. I'll give you choices, variations of the postures along the way. In every pose, find that place where you feel a good stretch. Go into every posture, they're called asanas, slowly. Leave every posture, every asana, slowly. Be your best friend."

Here, Eugenie paused, wondering why it wasn't in her to be her own best friend. But, like the expression goes, do what I say, not what I do.

Someone in the back said, "What about the saying, no pain, no gain?"

"Forget it," said Eugenie. "Probably spoken by an orthopedic surgeon and bet your bottom dollar, they were trying to drum up business. So, enough talk. Let's get going."

She warmed them up, focusing first on the neck, then shoulders. Cues for the postures she didn't do in her other classes came back to her and after a few minutes, the class was ready to do cat-cow asana.

Eugenie looked out at the group and said, "Focus first on your alignment on hands and knees in what is known as table top. Alignment's important in yoga as it keeps us safe and helps get the most out of the posture. Attend to your hands on the mat. Is there space between fingers with your middle finger pointing straight forward? Are your hands underneath your shoulders and are your knees underneath your hips? If so, begin the posture by inhaling through the nose and on your exhale through the mouth, curl the back up toward the sky. Then breathe in through the nose again as you bring your gaze forward, collarbone wide and neck long."

Spinal balance was next and after the position cue and reminder to hold for five breaths, a few groans could be heard.

"Challenging if we're not used to it," said Eugenie. "Give it time. You probably have noticed we sit a lot these days, what with commuting and work. That affects hips, legs, core, neck, and head."

"The new smoking, sitting is," someone said.

"I'm going to need help," someone else said.

Eugenie went to the student's side and guided her into position, all the while keeping an eye out on the rest of the class. This was the biggest challenge in teaching a large group. Everyone had different issues. Everyone was at a different level.

Feeling confident the student wouldn't hurt herself, Eugenie returned to the front of the class. "So downward dog, sound familiar?" Some nodded. Others looked blank. "Okay, let's review then after a few more poses, we'll go into savasana, which is relaxation stretched out, backs on the mat. First watch, here's downward dog."

From table top, Eugenie lifted her knees with her spine stretching out long and flat. Between her arms, her head and neck were relaxed, and her legs were hip distance apart. Her heels, she noted with some pride, were flat on the floor.

A good demonstration, she applauded herself. The only problem, she realized too late, was that her top had crept up her back. That, however, was nothing compared to what was happening in front. She gasped as she noticed her breasts had partially escaped the confines of the fabric. Quickly, she collapsed into child's pose, a curled ball on the mat.

This move served to hide her embarrassment but also confused the class, half of whom were now in child's pose and the other half in downward dog.

Eugenie stood up and saw in a mirror that her face was red. Best to get everyone into child's pose with their foreheads on the mat so they wouldn't notice.

"Considering that some are new to the practice," said Eugenie, trying to be cool as if this was the plan in the first place, "I'd thought I'd demonstrate child's pose. It's always an option for anyone anytime in class."

After a while, they got back to downward dog with some of the class struggling and others lifting one leg skyward as if there was no such thing as gravity.

Still, when Eugenie cued savasana, the relief from the entire class was palpable.

What she wasn't able to feel, she realized with dismay, was her own.

In the restroom after class, Eugenie locked the stall door and sat fully clothed on the toilet seat, hands over her head. She tried encouraging herself. After all, even though there were a few glitches, she had done it. Finished the class, check. Kept her word to Sarah, check. And without notes, which she'd forgotten in the car. Slowly, as she drank in the restroom's silence, she began to feel better.

That is, until the door to the hallway swung open, and voices erupted.

"She may not look much like a yogi, but I learned something. Like in alligator, how she had us squeeze elbows to ribs as we moved forward. That really helped."

"Well," began a second voice, "Don't get used to it. Sarah will be back next week. Unless…"

"She has another date," said a third voice.

"Date, my ass, that was a booty call," concluded a fourth. "Leave it to Jared."

Lowering her hands from her head, Eugenie bolted upright. So that was Sarah's motive to get out of teaching the class at the last moment. Eugenie felt ill, then angry. She'd been used. She reached behind herself and flushed as hard as she could. That did the trick. The voices stopped, the door opened then shut, and for a long time, there was silence.

When she was more than sure she was alone, Eugenie snuck out of the bathroom.

**5**

**"SO THAT WAS** a burger, right? Single or double?"

"A single," Eugenie said. "Wait! No, make that a double."

"With or without cheese?"

"Oh, with cheese, very much with cheese," said Eugenie.

"Will that complete your order?" the tinny voice asked, and Eugenie wondered by the strained politeness of the request if the employee had recently finished burger school 101.

"Yes," Eugenie replied then, "No! Make that with some fries, a large fries."

"Will you be eating at home or in the car?"

Oh, for pity sake, thought Eugenie, what business could it be of theirs? In the rear-view mirror, Eugenie could see a long line of cars. Arms out windows waved in impatience.

The voice in the box waited for a response and when there was none, continued, "Ma'am, we package the order differently depending on where you plan to eat."

"Car, make that car," said Eugenie.

"Thanks, you can pull up."

With the order of food warm in her lap, Eugenie found a tree in the large lot and parked under it. As she was about to take a bite out of the enormous burger, she saw the studio owner get out of a nearby car and head in her direction. Eugenie didn't hesitate. She threw the burger back into the bag and covered it with a raincoat she found in the back seat. Then she opened all the windows wide just in time to come eye to eye with Martha.

"Hey...you," said Martha. "Come to this plaza often? The home goods store is one of my favorites. Is it possible for one person to have too many accent pillows? That scoundrel Nandy has left her mark on every single one. Is there a support group for someone who can't resist buying another pillow?"

Laughing politely at Martha's joke, Eugenie surveyed the stores in the strip mall and pointed, "The shoe repair shop, I go there."

Martha peered down at Eugenie's feet. "Flip flops giving you fits?"

"Some heels I wear occasionally. And a Mary Jane that needed a new buckle," Eugenie said, now on a roll. "Then there was that pair of boots with a wonky zipper. I'm here a lot," she said and swallowed. "It's not so unusual to see me here."

Martha looked around. "Can you believe the odor from that burger joint? All the way over here, I can smell it. Can you?"

Eugenie flattened her hand against the raincoat. "Now that you mention it, yes, I can."

Martha shook her head. "If you ask me, no different than eating our dogs. And will you look at the line around that place? When there's a better way, it's so sad."

Eugenie did her best to put on a sympathetic face, but Martha was on to the next subject. "So, ethics..."

Here it comes, thought Eugenie.

"Ethics?" Eugenie repeated weakly, her hand pressing down even harder on the raincoat, now fanned out against the passenger seat.

"You've seen the email?" said Martha. "The one that says the practice alliance has required an ethics class for teachers in order to renew their certification?"

"Oh, that email," Eugenie nodded, trying to remember the last time she had opened her account.

"So cut to the chase," said Martha. "I've scheduled it for next week. Wednesday at 7. Teachers from other studios have been invited too. Get there early if you want a good seat on the floor."

"Will do," Eugenie said, letting out a sigh of relief. "You can count on me."

"I know that," said Martha. "Nobody needs an ethics class less than you."

# 6

**SHE WOULD FIND** a 9-5 job, Eugenie thought to herself, or more accurately, a proper job. A job at one of those big box stores where everyone's BMI was out of range and not on the skinny side. To her fellow employees, she would seem impossibly slim, and they would say things like, "Eugenie, you can squeeze into that space," or "Eugenie, you can climb that ladder, no problem." Or perhaps, "If anyone can fit into those jeans, it's Eugenie."

In the big box world, her weight and eating habits would not bother people and, if a topic of discussion at all, would only be to her advantage. Maybe at lunch she could even eat a burger without apology.

Or... she could remain a yoga teacher and not care.

Wasn't that the whole point of yoga? The yoking of mind, body, and spirit, which pointed to what? Freedom! Freedom with burgers or without burgers - that's what she craved. So, go ahead, talk about me all you want. It's not my business what you think of me (here she knew she was quoting some guru or other). Energized by the thought, she reached out for the food which lay in ruins beside her and as it turned out; she wasn't hungry anyway, so there. She took a deep breath and noticed, for the first time, an insistent rumble off in the distance and air, thick with moisture, seeping in through the windows of the car.

"The usual pattern is not taking hold quite yet," the forecaster on the TV declared that morning. Eugenie had lived in the area long enough to know what that meant. Rain could and did arrive at any time. Not a great idea to have all the windows down, so she engaged the car's electrical system, and brought them up. None too soon, for in the next instant, a deluge engulfed the vehicle, turning the world outside the windshield blurry and dim. Even the lights from the strip mall were hard to pick out. From every direction, there was thunder, and in the dampness of the car, she shivered.

She turned the key in the ignition, then changed her mind. Driving in this mess wasn't the smartest plan. Better to stay put.

She moved to get comfortable in the seat but was interrupted by a scream coming from somewhere outside the car. Eugenie peered through the glass but could see nothing but fuzzy shapes. Again, she tried to settle in, but this time, it was laughter that caught her attention. Everything's okay, she reassured herself. Someone had probably misjudged the depth of a puddle and gotten soaked.

The surrounding storm continued with a vengeance. The thunder was so loud, she could barely hear herself think. Maybe she should call someone. Her housemate? No, she had read it was a bad idea to use a cell phone in a storm unless you had to. And Arabelle, Eugenie reminded herself, had not shone herself to be the warm and cozy type.

A loud knock on the window made her jump.

"Eugenie! Is that you? It's me, Jared."

"What the...," she said, thinking she must be imagining things.

The pounding, now fierce, continued. "Eugenie, please, it's Jared, let me in." She saw a figure dash in front of the windshield, then tug at the car door. "Eugenie!"

Finger on the lock release, Eugenie hesitated. A spurned girlfriend (if only she could call herself that!) would not let this, let's be clear, character in. His yoga teacher, however, would. She unlocked the door.

"Shit!" he said, jumping into the passenger seat. "Took you long enough."

She looked at him, taking comfort in the fact he was soaked to the bones. "How did you know it was me in here?" she finally said.

"Recognized the car. Seen you walk to it enough times after class. What're you doing anyways, out in this storm?"

She considered answering, then decided because she had given him shelter, she didn't owe him anything more. "More to the point," she said, "What're you doing out in this parking lot?"

"Car's a piece of shit," said Jared. "Shuddered like a high rise in a quake at the last intersection. Barely made it into the lot before it died. Tow truck on the way."

"May be hours before it shows up," Eugenie observed, trying hard not to smile.

"You're telling me," said Jared. Then I saw your car and thought..."

"What? Thought what?" asked Eugenie.

"I don't know, luck of the Irish," said Jared.

"You're hardly Irish," said Eugenie.

"Full of blarney though," Jared snorted, swatting at a pant leg. When water splashed back in his face, he sighed, "Shit, I'm baked."

"You kidding me?" said Eugenie.

"Ah, lay off," said Jared. "Just take me home. It's not far. Otherwise, I'll be stuck waiting for the tow. Like you said, could be hours. In these clothes, I'll catch the plague or pneumonia. Syphilis. Something! C'mon."

By then the storm had subsided and the last words of his plea came out loud and clear. Since they no longer had to shout to be heard, she figured now was the time to get out and walk. She was about to suggest it when lightning struck a lamppost not a hundred feet away. A spectacular flash lit up the interior of the car, revealing a defeated Jared sitting on a wrinkled raincoat with a bag of fast food dangling from the sleeve. In the next instant, the lights of the parking lot went out. And therefore, walking was out as well.

She sighed and turned the key in the ignition. "In the state you're in, you shouldn't be driving anyway. What were you thinking?"

Beside her, he sunk down further in the seat. "I was thinking," he began, his voice barely audible. "I was thinking, and God strike me dead if I'm lying, I might run into you."

**GIVEN HIS CONDITION,** it was a miracle Jared remembered the code that opened the sub-division gate. And then the house number, another miracle. "My area code when I was a kid," he said.

She drove a few miles down a deserted winding street lined with matching mailboxes, then pulled into the stone-flagged driveway. The rain had stopped and the view out the windshield was clear. "Wow," she said and when he didn't answer, she repeated softly to herself, "Wow."

The house, complete with circular driveway, Greek columns, and orchestrated landscaping, was as big as castles she'd seen in photographs. The lighting was impressive, showing off every palm and oak tree to perfection. Glistening raindrops sparkled like diamonds and added to the effect. Not able to help herself, she said for a third time, "Wow." Then she remembered Jared and gave him a nudge. "We're here."

Nothing from the passenger seat. She nudged him again, this time harder. "Jared!"

Finally, there was a grunt, followed by something incomprehensible. Then, without warning, Jared shot straight up, smashing his head against the roof of the car. It looked like it hurt, but to her surprise, he burst out laughing.

"Geez, Jared," said Eugenie. "We're here. Time for bed."

The fast-food bag under him crinkled as he lunged toward her. "Sounds good to me," he said.

His state, altered as it was, failed at first to register the expression on her face. Then slowly, it sunk in. As if to pacify his disappointment, he leaned in the opposite direction, and spent a few moments carefully choosing from the mess that lay crushed and wet under his shoes - a single French fry. Eugenie watched as he popped it into his mouth.

She continued to stare in amazement until her attention was drawn to an old woman who had exited the house. With surprisingly brisk footsteps, she walked to the passenger side of the car and proceeded to tap, gently but firmly, on the window. Jared groaned, but after several tries, he managed to open the door. Acknowledging Eugenie with a brief nod, the woman guided Jared into the house.

By the efficiency of her movements and the compliance of his, it was as if it had all been done many times before.

**8**

**"SO, WHAT HAVE** we here? A chaturanga if my eyes don't deceive?"

"Arabelle!" said Eugenie, collapsing to the rug on the living room floor. "You scared the hell out of me! I thought you were at work."

"Mental health day," said Arabelle. "I'm taking one. But I'm right, aren't I? That is what you were doing."

Eugenie rolled onto her side, propping her head up with one hand. "Yes, chaturanga. In English, alligator pose."

"Makes sense," said Arabelle. "Long and low. Looks like an alligator, not that I've ever seen one."

"Live here long enough and you might," said Eugenie. "Speaking of which, how long are you going to be living here?"

Arabelle took a swig of liquid from the mug she was carrying. "You in a hurry to get rid of me?"

"No," said Eugenie. "The rent you pay helps. Just curious."

To Eugenie's surprise, Arabelle joined her on the floor.

"So how do you teach chaturanga to a beginner, to a beginning student, if you were going to," asked Arabelle.

"You really interested in trying?" said Eugenie.

"The day needs something new, I figure," said Arabelle.

"You want to talk about it?" said Eugenie.

"Not really," Arabelle said, pointing. "Show me where to put arms and legs like I was in class."

"You could come to class," said Eugenie.

"Not happening," said Arabelle.

"Okay then, chaturanga, alligator pose," said Eugenie. "Here's how."

Positioning her body in an upside-down V, Eugenie explained, "From downward dog you bring yourself forward into plank, like when you were in school, and you were about to do a boy's push-up."

"Maybe like when you were in school. For kicks, show me the girl's version," said Arabelle.

"Can do." From full plank, Eugenie put her knees down and looked at Arabelle. "Engage your belly muscles, then come forward, elbows pressed against ribs, shoulders and arms working hard, and put your head down, like this."

"As if the alligator is getting ready to devour something," said Arabelle.

"Exactly, now you," said Eugenie.

With no trouble Arabelle got herself into downward dog, then into plank with knees down on the rug. Ever so slowly, she moved forward to the floor position and ended with her forehead on the rug.

"Impressive. Sure this is your first time trying?" said Eugenie. "I didn't see an arm shake on the way into position, nothing. And your breathing..."

"What about my breathing?" said Arabelle.

"Well, they say a seasoned practitioner is one whose breathing never varies from pose to pose or within a pose," said Eugenie. "And you say you've never done this before?"

Arabelle was already back on her feet, mug in hand. "Must have been my emotional state, if you know what I mean. Fueling the fire."

"I completely get what you mean," Eugenie said, about to tell her the events of last night. But Arabelle had already retreated to her room, the door shut quietly behind her.

**9**

**A BELL, SIGNALING** the end to the meditation session, went off on Eugenie's phone app. Fifteen minutes had gone by and not once did her mind find anything close to nothingness. Instead, there had been to-do lists, revisits of meaningless conversations, and the persistent opening of that door in her brain which never failed to dump every fault she had in a heap on the floor. Although only in her mind's eye, she could make out every fault.

Your weight is an issue, Eugenie. It makes people think and say you do not look like a yoga instructor.

You had a one-night stand and with a student, Eugenie.

You probably need to get a proper job, Eugenie.

And some new yoga clothes. Clothes that fit better. With more sophisticated patterns, hell, with any pattern. Your students need something interesting to look at when you're up there teaching. As for your house, it's seriously in need of a de-clutter. And before the heat outside rivals Hades, the air conditioner needs a checkup. And on and on and on. Until at last, a Denzge bell, tuned to an ancient note signifying an unknown meaning, announced it was time to stop. The app followed with the message: "Well done! You, along with 4358 others, can check meditation off your list for today."

But no, meditation could not be checked off, not today, not yet. She set the timer on start. Once again, the beginning bell went off, followed by the sound of a male voice chanting "Om," joined in quick succession by a host of other voices. Who were these men? she wondered. Were they monks? They sounded like monks, like they believed, like they were believers. The thought reassured her. Then she thought, no, get real Eugenie. They were probably contract singers, hired for an hourly rate, a small sum to augment their pay from performing in off-off-off Broadway musicals. Therefore, she concluded, they were only being paid to sound like they believed. That, too, irritated her. Was nothing what it seemed in life? The end bell went off. She grunted, opened her eyes to set the timer, and once more the voices began.

Less than a minute in, the sound of the refrigerator dwarfed the chant and Eugenie could not help but wonder, had the refrigerator ever sounded this loud? Maybe it was getting old, ready to quit. How old was it anyway, five years, ten years? Had her parents had it when she and Tom got married?

And speaking of Tom, what was he doing these days? Some people kept in touch after divorcing. Some even stayed friends. Definitely not the case with her and Tom. A thought struck: if Tom could see her with Jared, oh, that would be lovely, the sweetest revenge. Tom admired athletes and even an injured one would make an impression.

The bell went off again and this time she punched the timer so hard, the phone flew out of her hand. Groaning, she reminded herself she would be calm, she would breathe. If it killed her, she would. She yawned and then forced her mouth shut, and then, because the yawn had been cut short, yawned again. By now one of her knees hurt and she reacted by curling onto her side and placing a pillow under her head. Instead of helping her focus, the position triggered sleep. She only woke when the alarm went off again. Looking at the time, she realized she had slept through more than an hour of ringing bells. She stood up and stretched, feeling more tired than she had in months. Knocking gently on Arabelle's door, she heard no response. She knocked louder, then twisted the knob. The room was empty, Arabelle nowhere in sight.

Sighing, Eugenie shut the door. If mental health was to be had this day, it wouldn't be in this house.

**"SO ETHICS, WHAT** does it mean?" Martha asked, infusing the question with her usual verve.

The group of twenty-some teachers facing her remained silent. From their lack of response, it wasn't clear if they were trying to get comfortable on mats or if they were at a loss to answer.

Eugenie wasn't at a loss. She knew exactly what ethics were. And what they weren't. She busied herself by pretending to turn the volume off on her phone.

Finally, someone raised a hand. "It's hot in here and stuffy. Possible to crank up the air?"

Martha nodded, scooting out of the room in the direction of the studio thermostat. Nandy, who'd been at Martha's side, got up and bypassed several rows of teachers to find Eugenie.

"Why, Nandy girl, hello," said Eugenie, stroking the dog's soft fur. Then, out of the corner of her eye, she saw Jared through the open door. He glanced briefly in the room, then disappeared. From the parking lot came the sound of a car engine revving.

Martha returned, her mood bearing no semblance to the one she'd had when she'd left. She did not look happy, and Eugenie surmised it was not because the teachers were slow to answer what ethics were.

"I found the back door propped open again," she said, looking out at the group. "Again! Why?"

On the mats, no one stirred.

"Okay, since no one's going to fess up," said Martha, "The back door is never, I repeat, never to be propped open. Air conditioning for a place like this costs a fortune. Even you people from other studios must know that. And Nandy might... Speaking of which, where is...?"

"Here, Martha," said Eugenie. "She's right here."

"Thank heaven," Martha said. "Come here Nandy."

The dog, curled in a tight ball by Eugenie's side, didn't move.

"Nandy, come here now," said Martha.

On the mat, Eugenie distanced herself slightly from the dog. The creature didn't move.

"Nandy!" admonished Martha.

By this time, the class had turned in Eugenie's direction, their eyes pleading with her to release whatever hold she had on the dog so they could get this ethics thing over. But now a full-fledged power struggle was in play. With a loud whack! Martha's palm slammed on the floor.

"Nandy," Martha whispered over the silence of the room.

Only the sound of the dog's breathing, rhythmic and undisturbed in sleep, answered back.

Glaring, Martha switched her focus to Eugenie. In a flash, Eugenie picked up Nandy, crossed the room, and deposited her gently by Martha's side. The relaxation of the class was palpable.

Martha, clutching the dog tight in her lap, looked out at the group. "So, ethics," she began again. "The study of right and wrong. Not foreign to yoga, part of the eight limbs, right? Known as the observances and restraints."

The yoga teachers nodded tentatively, but no one dared speak.

Frustrated, Martha sighed and said, "Okay, let's start with the restraints. This is easy. What could a yoga teacher do that's wrong?"

Bodies shifted on the mats. Then, from the corner of the room, a raised hand. It was Sarah's.

"Touch a student inappropriately, you know, not getting permission first," said Sarah.

Eugenie lowered her chin, swallowing the urge to react. Sarah sure as hell had gotten permission from Jared, so no problem there. Then, curious what the others might be thinking, Eugenie looked around the room and saw many knowing smiles.

For the moment, it seemed, the study of ethics had been mastered.

## 11

**AFTER THE CLASS,** which lasted to the minute a full hour, there would be no quick exit. From the departing group of teachers, Martha pulled Eugenie aside, her fingers lingering like an indictment on the soft flesh above Eugenie's elbow.

Between them on the floor, Nandy nuzzled an ear against Eugenie's ankle. Without thinking, Eugenie picked the dog up. The small lines on Martha's forehead deepened and Eugenie quickly handed over the dog. Clearing her throat a little louder than she intended, Eugenie asked, "Will this take long? I think I'm coming down with something."

Martha stepped back. The move was slight, and in her arms, Nandy failed to move with her. Instead, the small wet nose pulled toward Eugenie.

"Not long, no," Martha said, looking at the dog. "You haven't given anything to Nandy, I hope, in the way of food, that is?"

"No," Eugenie said, and despite her innocence, she felt a blush come to her cheeks.

"No, you wouldn't," said Martha. "She trusts you."

There was a long silence as Martha pressed a proprietary hand against the squirming dog.

Then finally, Martha added, "As do your students."

"That's nice to know," said Eugenie, thinking the owner's words sounded more like a threat than a statement of fact.

"Jared was here," said Martha. "Did you see? A private lesson."

"Good for him," said Eugenie.

"Good for the studio, too," said Martha. "He has a lot of connections."

"I would guess," said Eugenie.

"He talked about your class," said Martha.

"Ah," said Eugenie.

"How you inspired him," said Martha.

"Oh?" said Eugenie.

"To want more," said Martha.

Eugenie coughed. It was a loose phlegmy sound, and she thanked her body for producing it.

"So, I wanted to take a few moments to let you know that," said Martha, holding the dog even closer as she turned. Over her shoulder, she added, "Get some rest for that cough. No teacher, no class, no good, I always say."

In the car, the same phlegm which had served to prove a point now marinated in an empty stomach and Eugenie began to think she really was sick. By the time she lifted the toilet seat at home, there was no doubt.

## 12

**SOMEONE HAD LEFT** two messages on Eugenie's phone, but in her funk, she struggled to place the name.

Then she remembered. Of course, Ralph, from the studio. When she'd first heard the name, so close to a bark, it sounded harsh against the peace of the studio. She vaguely remembered that he'd been the one who handed her employment papers to fill out. That day he introduced himself not as Martha's husband but as the "IT guy around here, the one who keeps the website going, who tracks usage of class passes. The one who orders printer ink, you know, high-level stuff."

Like Eugenie, Ralph had a round face. Taking the forms from him that day, she found herself, having recognized a mutual carnivore, smiling widely. He responded warmly but briefly, and for a few moments, she entertained some distinctly lustful thoughts.

It was not until the Christmas party, when both a little drunk and squeezed into the back hallway of Martha's house, he confessed his marriage to the studio owner.

"I'm Martha's fourth, at least I think I am," said Ralph to Eugenie. "Corner her in this crowd...who the hell are all these people, anyway? She might admit to a fifth. She calls me George when she's horny, sometimes Felipe when she's ready to go off."

"That can't make you happy," Eugenie responded and, in her disappointment at the news, she took a long swig of wine.

"Happy? No, then I remember the perks of the job. And it really is a job I was hired for. Martha couldn't afford to pay me for what I do in the studio. A husband was much cheaper."

"How...," Eugenie began.

"Sad," Ralph finished. "That's what you were going to say, weren't you? I can see you're a romantic, even worse, an idealist. Has the practice of yoga not taught you anything?"

Eugenie had had too much to drink, and the remark stung. Leaving his side, she pushed against the crowd till she finally found a way out the front door. In the fresh air, she placed the wine glass, still clenched in her fist, bottoms up in a flower planter. She walked the ten blocks home.

Remembering the scene, she felt the nausea of last night return. She found an open ginger ale can in the refrigerator and downed the stale contents. A few crackers followed and soon, blood sugar restored, she felt better.

She called the number Ralph had left, and the studio picked up. The person at the desk, someone by the name of Daisy whom Eugenie had not met, much less heard of, said Ralph had gone and no, she did not know where or when he could be reached.

**13**

**THE FOLLOWING DAY** at the studio, Eugenie entered the classroom where she was scheduled to teach to find it full of boxes. She didn't expect the class to be large, but still. She went out to the desk to inquire.

A toothy smile met her question. "You must be Eugenie."

It annoyed Eugenie that whoever this was knew who she was. She could imagine how she was described. "Eugenie's easy to pick out. She's the one that doesn't look like a yoga teacher."

Turning this over in her mind, Eugenie paused. Finally, her words came out: "There are boxes in the small studio."

"Yes, we're growing!" the eager face replied.

"I don't think my class will have enough room," said Eugenie.

"All for the sake of progress!"

Eugenie took a deep breath. "I'm sorry... you are?"

"Daisy, glad to meet you. I've always wanted to work at a yoga studio, and well, here I am. Don't let anyone tell you dreams don't come true. They do if I'm anything to go by, and I am, don't you think?"

"What I think is that there won't be enough space in that room to teach," said Eugenie.

"Flexibility!" said Daisy. "Isn't that what yoga's all about?"

"Then you're saying another space is available?" said Eugenie. "I thought the other rooms were taken."

"Right," agreed Daisy. "All taken."

"So that leaves me up... shit creek," Eugenie almost said, then remembered where she was.

Around the corner, Martha appeared, Nandy in her arms. "Children," she said, "Play nice. Whatever is the matter?"

Daisy began to answer and Eugenie, with no goodwill left, cut her off. "There are boxes in the small studio."

"We are growing," Martha said.

Nandy, having squirmed out of Martha's grasp, busied herself rubbing against Eugenie's ankles. Eugenie picked the dog up, saw Martha's expression, then returned the dog to the floor. Questions from what was in the boxes to why they weren't placed somewhere reasonable, like a closet or a storage unit, were left unasked.

"You see, growing! I was right!" beamed Daisy from behind the desk. Eugenie weighed whether biting any harder on her tongue would bring blood.

"Do what you can," Martha said. "I have faith."

"We can rely on this one," chimed in Daisy. "She's the person we can count on around here to cover for classes at the last minute, or whatever else is needed."

"And you would know that how?" Eugenie asked.

"The first task of the new hire," said Daisy. "Get to know what's going on."

"Good. Excellent," said Eugenie, taking in a deep breath. "Then maybe you would know why Ralph tried to get in touch with me yesterday."

"No idea, sorry," Daisy replied, and simultaneously, Martha said, "Ralph?"

"Yes," Eugenie replied. "Ralph. Twice."

Martha picked up Nandy, who was now asleep on Eugenie's feet, and declared, "I'm sure it was nothing."

Daisy straightened to her full height and said to Martha's back, "But if it was nothing, why would he make it a point to call?"

Good question, thought Eugenie, returning to her class, which in the end, worked out. A handful of students showed up, and she changed the sequencing so that postures could be done without coming into contact with a wall or cardboard.

The next day, the boxes were gone.

# 14

**SO WAS DAISY,** proving that it was not done to get ahead of Martha. There were now two new people at the desk. Both looked blank as Eugenie asked about a discrepancy in a recent paycheck.

"Martha can help you with that," one offered tentatively.

"I believe you could, too," said Eugenie, handing over a piece of paper. "Check what's in the computer for that class."

One of the new hires directed fierce attention to the paper then the screen. "That was a Friday?"

"Yes," said Eugenie, "A Friday."

"It's coming up," the new hire said with relief. "And what is it you need?"

"The class count," said Eugenie.

"Okay, class count, let me see. Yes, there it is. Eleven. Eleven clients in that class."

"The payroll breakdown I received showed nine," said Eugenie.

The new hire struggled to understand. "So, not eleven?"

"No, not eleven," said Eugenie. "Nine."

"And...?"

"And that's important because teachers are paid per client," said Eugenie.

The new hire chewed on a long piece of hair. "So...," she said.

"So," said Eugenie, "I was underpaid by two clients."

"Oh, I see!" the new hire responded, eyebrows raised in triumph.

"It needs to be corrected in my next paycheck," said Eugenie.

"Martha could do that."

"But not you?" asked Eugenie.

"Definitely not me," said the one new hire, while the other nodded vigorously.

"Is Martha in the studio?" asked Eugenie.

"Ocupado," said the other new hire, speaking for the first time.

Eugenie was beginning to lose patience. "I beg your pardon?"

"She's here, but busy. Private lesson."

"Could you leave her a note to talk to me?" said Eugenie. "I'll be in the library."

One new hire turned to the other. "There's a library here? Don't remember that on the tour."

"It's before the utility closet, by the herbal tea," said Eugenie. "There's a door."

"I remember that door. We didn't go through it. Martha never told us we could go through it."

"Well, if you did," said Eugenie, "You would find the library. It's small, more of a large closet if you want to know the truth."

"Maybe Martha didn't think we'd need the library. That's why she didn't show us."

To this, Eugenie could find no words, so after a few moments of silence from both sides of the desk, Eugenie said, "Anyway, that's where I'll be. If you could tell her."

"Oh yes," they both answered in unison.

Eugenie walked away feeling as though she could be in the library until the cows came home, and never would Martha be told to find her there.

## 15

**IT WAS ONE** of her favorite places in the world, this library, and her foul mood, try as she might to hold on to it, disappeared. Next to a bookshelf, she found a soft embroidered cushion. She turned on a reading lamp and settled in. From a small stool, she picked up a book.

It was by one of those gurus who had gotten himself in trouble. Something about a hoard of luxury cars. Still, Eugenie had always loved his writings. Inhaling the soft scent of sandalwood which hung in the air, she felt the weight of the book in her hands and stared at his photo on the cover.

He had a twinkle in his eye, which the first time she saw it, seemed to have something to do with enlightenment, but the more she found out about him, probably had to do with an appreciation for world-class engineering, which promised a uniformly quiet ride.

She opened the book to no particular page and read: "Life is not something to be solved. To look at it like you would try to solve a problem is to take a wrong approach."

If she were honest with herself, she had taken quite a few wrong approaches lately, for there were many problems, one being that she was not being paid accurately by the studio. Today was the first time it had dawned on her to check the payroll breakdown, and she wondered if discrepancies had happened before.

What was the current thinking about yoga teachers, that they were flaky? In her case, possibly true, for since the beginning of her employment, she had adopted what could only be described as an indifferent attitude toward her pay.

Clearly, that had to change. From now on, she would confirm the student count and insist on being paid what she was due.

And speaking of money, what about what Arabelle was paying her for the room? Was Eugenie getting anywhere near the value of what she was providing? She had to admit she had not done more than slapdash research to see what that might be. She hadn't even asked Arabelle to sign a lease.

Eugenie turned off the lamp and put the book aside. These things, and others, she would meditate on. She set the timer on her phone, and the soft sound of "Om" filled the small space.

Barely a minute into the session, the library door opened wide, hitting the wall Eugenie leaned against with a loud thump. Startled, she fell off the cushion.

"They said I might find you here," said Martha, flipping on the overhead fixture. "Something about the count."

Eugenie blinked a few times to adjust to the light.

"Well, I'm waiting," Martha said.

Try as she might, and focused as she was on no thought, Eugenie could not remember what it was she was going to ask regarding the count. "Ah...," she said, bargaining for time.

"I have a private session to get to," said Martha. "After that, you know where to find me."

Eugenie continued to search her brain. "Now I remember!" she declared, but it was too late. Martha was on to the next subject. "Could you shelve this?" she said, holding a book in her hand. "But before you do, take a peek. It might be of interest."

Alone again in the library, Eugenie peered down at the cover and shook her head.

It was, to no one's surprise, least of all her own, a book on dieting.

# 16

**"YOU WANT FRIES** with that?" said the voice.

"Hell yes," said Eugenie. "Make it two, no, three orders."

"Will you be eating...?"

"In the car, yes," said Eugenie. "Packaged to be eaten while in a car. A Toyota if it's any of your business."

"No," said the efficient voice, "Doesn't matter what the brand of car. We only need to know if you'll be eating in the car or at home. Though I have to say Toyota is a good brand. My Dad drives a Toyota."

"Swell," Eugenie said, then waited for the total. But no luck. Apparently, they were still on the topic of cars.

"Something about engine life," offered the voice in the box.

"How much?" asked Eugenie.

"Geez, over 25 grand, that's for sure."

"No," said Eugenie. "My order. The food. How much?"

Eugenie paid, took the bags, and pulled over to park. She hadn't gotten the burger packaging all the way open when a loud knock on the window stopped her.

On the windshield leaned Jared, offering an expensive smile, his teeth having been whitened to perfection. Before she had time to react, he was in the passenger seat.

"You following me?" Eugenie said with a glare.

"No, I saw you leave the studio," said Jared.

"Meaning yes," said Eugenie.

"Hey, I was in the studio legitimately," said Jared. "I needed to use the facilities."

"You couldn't use them at home?" Eugenie asked.

"You questioning my habits, my small bladder, what?" said Jared. "I needed to go, so I stopped."

"You high?" asked Eugenie.

"You suspicious?" responded Jared.

"Yeah, I guess you could say so," said Eugenie.

"Got any to share?" he pointed toward the bags.

She handed both over to him.

"Yum," he said, taking a large bite of burger, "Hits the spot. You not hungry?"

"Not anymore," Eugenie said.

"Another, a different appetite kicked in?" said Jared.

To her irritation, Eugenie felt herself blush. "Let's say I remember a few things."

"I remember a few things, too," he said, finishing the last of the burger. "Let's go to your place."

"No, yours," Eugenie said. "It isn't far."

"The maids are all over it," said Jared, shaking his head.

"I have a tenant," said Eugenie, "Remember?"

"She have a job?" asked Jared.

"Downtown, I think. Actually, I'm not sure," said Eugenie.

"Let's pretend it is," Jared said, leaning forward to kiss her lips. "That way roomie has a long commute."

**THE NEXT DAY** Eugenie found herself in an especially good mood, and she tried hard not to think about the reason. When a student in class asked about the sutras, she was surprised to hear her voice shake.

After a pause and clearing of the throat, Eugenie answered, "Sutras are teachings. And one big takeaway is regarding attachment and how it's connected to suffering."

"Attachment to?" asked a student from the back row.

"Good question," said Eugenie. "What are those things we're attached to?"

"Our stuff," offered one student.

"Definitely," responded Eugenie. "Like?"

"My pool with jacuzzi."

There was laughter around the room, and someone added, "The dog with the big bucks' pedigree."

"My new car, a Lexus." The group was getting into it.

"My address, the gated community where I live."

This was one privileged gathering, thought Eugenie. She looked out at their eager faces. "Okay, let's make it more personal. What about our bodies?"

"The way we look," answered Sarah, who, for some reason, had decided to take Eugenie's class. Eugenie watched as Sarah leaped up from her mat and pretended to showcase the way her tights and top clung to her curves. The class howled with laughter.

"Yes," said Eugenie, at the same time wondering if anyone was getting the point. The discussion had turned into an attachment celebration.

"Let's make it even more personal," continued Eugenie. "What else are we attached to?"

The door Eugenie had taken time to close at the beginning of class, now opened, and in stepped Jared. Did she imagine it, or was the reaction of the gathered a sigh of lust?

She tried, unsuccessfully, to tamp down her rage. The man had no shame. He knew the rules as well as anyone, the first being that in this yoga studio, a shut door means the class has started.

As expected, Jared's presence didn't fail to distract. Someone asked Eugenie to repeat the question.

"No problem," answered Eugenie, feeling nothing like her words implied. "What are we most attached to?"

"Our...," someone began, then paused, "Desires," and the class shrieked. Once again, Eugenie could not keep herself from blushing, and she tucked her head in a manner anyone looking at her would think distinctly uncomfortable.

"Reproduction of the species!" another student replied.

"A more personal attachment than that," Eugenie said, raising her voice to be heard above the din of the room.

By the door, Jared, still standing, no mat in hand, giving no clue as to what he was doing there, cleared his throat.

The room quieted and seemed to hold its collective breath.

"Our individual lives," he said, grinning at the group, then focusing on Eugenie, he said, "My life."

## 18

**EUGENIE MANAGED TO** make it out of the studio before tears flowed. Trying to remember where she parked her car, she failed and was left to stare stupidly at her cell phone, which continued to sound out the playlist. As she juggled it along with keys and flip flops, her mat slipped from her hands.

Out of the corner of one wet eye, she saw a hand reaching toward her. "Here," said a voice.

It was Ralph. She blinked several times and wiped at her cheeks, but it was no use. He had seen.

"My car...," Eugenie said.

"Something happen to your car?" he asked.

"No," Eugenie said. "Yes. I mean, probably not. I can't remember where I parked it."

"Come to mine," said Ralph. "It's right here. For a moment. Until you've..."

"Recovered," she knew he was going to say, but he corrected in time to say, "Remembered."

In the vehicle, an expensive sporty type made smaller by all the stuff in it, Ralph rummaged for a tissue. After a few seconds, he gave up. "I know, I know. It looks like I live here. Well, someways I do. No tissue, but hey, you can use my sleeve."

Eugenie's self-esteem had vanished, and with it, her pride. She took him up on the offer. "Thanks," she said, wiping her face.

For several moments, the two sat, looking out the windshield. A security guard walked by and slowed, giving them the once-over. Ralph gave a small wave. The guard saluted back and continued on her way.

"There's a lot of security around this place," said Eugenie. "Something up?"

"Not that I know of," said Ralph. "But hey, if the stores think there's a need, I have no problem with it. Guards are friendly enough," he said, then paused. "You want to talk about it?"

She clutched her mat to her chest. "You're nice. Martha's lucky."

"I'm not sure," said Ralph. "We're very different people."

"Opposites attract, hmm?" Eugenie said, then coughed softly. "Does it seem that in yoga world, everyone is so perfect?"

The security guard was back again, this time tapping on the glass by Ralph's side. He opened the window.

"There have been reports of suspicious activity in the area," the guard began, then handed Ralph a wrinkled copy of a photograph. "Ever see this person?"

"Hard to tell," he said, handing it over to Eugenie. "Not exactly the clearest image."

"Best we got," said the guard.

Eugenie glanced at the photo, shook her head, then handed it back to Ralph, who gave it to the guard.

"Well, let me know if you see anything," the guard concluded, and turned to walk a diagonal path across the parking lot.

Eugenie watched her, then pointed. "Oh, there, I see it, my car. I better go."

"Sure?" said Ralph. "You okay to drive?"

"Yes, thanks," said Eugenie. "Forget what I said, one of those days."

"Already forgotten," said Ralph, then he got out of the car and ran around to open her door. For a second time that morning, she felt tears come to her eyes, and she looked away. She couldn't remember the last time anyone had done that.

## 19

**THE HOUSE WAS** quiet and had been for hours. Early on, Arabelle could be heard trying not to make noise in the kitchen, and then all went still. Too lazy to get out of bed, Eugenie stared at the bedroom ceiling and wondered again about her housemate.

The day Arabelle arrived at Eugenie's door, the woman had said something about responding to a message board notice regarding a room for rent. Eugenie was so engrossed in trying to remember where and when she had posted that notice, she only took in part of Arabelle's story. Something about being a traveling replacement for jobs that had yet to be filled permanently. Eugenie nodded, though she was clueless about what kind of jobs those might be. Rather than ask any more questions, Eugenie studied Arabelle's determined face and tall frame. There was something about the even features and the quietness of Arabelle's footfalls, which Eugenie trusted. Going down the hallway to show Arabelle her room, Eugenie only heard her own steps even though Arabelle was the one with shoes on. The deal was sealed when Arabelle gave Eugenie cash for the first and last month, explaining that with her job, it made no sense to open a checking account. She moved in that very day, bringing little luggage and even less company.

It was like living with a panther.

Over the coming weeks, Eugenie watched as Arabelle changed her toothbrush regularly and her towels every other day. The extra laundry wasn't a problem, as Arabelle occasionally added Eugenie's load to hers. However, the extra water might be an issue, and Eugenie reminded herself she should review the rent Arabelle paid.

But for now, meditation took precedence. As her tenant couldn't provide an excuse to delay, Eugenie searched for another. She was more aware than she would have liked that she was procrastinating, and after some minutes, she began to ask herself the cause. She quickly realized that meditation loomed as a pit where she might and probably would get stuck. This was not the first time that had happened, and she knew the answer was to start and face the pit.

To her relief, as she entered the kitchen, a curious sound from the refrigerator began. Grateful for any excuse to avoid meditation, Eugenie opened the refrigerator door and leaned in. The gauge was exactly as she remembered setting it, and the small thermometer she'd purchased read 38 degrees. Okay, cross off temperature being an issue. She was about to close the door when the sight of Arabelle's handwriting drew her attention.

The carefully shaped cursive took up every inch of the slip of a note and read, "Breakfast quiche, made this morning. All yours, the rest went to work." Another reason to delay, thought Eugenie gratefully, as she grabbed a slice and took a bite.

Then quickly gagged. The quiche had only touched her tongue when it became clear this was what might be called a healthy option quiche. Nothing close to actual egg or cheese or bacon was involved. So that's what accounted for Arabelle's lanky build: she was a vegan.

As if in spite, the refrigerator quieted down, and once again, there was no excuse not to meditate. She reached for her phone, opened the app, and set the timer. The familiar chant began. She connected to her breathing, noticing as it went in then out, in then out. Nothing came forth but a vague sense of doom.

She decided to review her life. Were her bills paid? Mostly. Was her sleep good? Rarely. Did she reach out to friends? Sort of, if texts counted. Was she eating more than she should? Yes, but that was normal. Would she substitute the quiche Arabelle had made for a fast-food binge? Totally, but that too was normal. Were her classes going well? If the happy nods meant anything, that would be a yes. Was the recycling separated, were the hedges trimmed, were the neighbors waved to? No, no, and no. Therefore, status normal. Everything was per usual, and yet...

She reset the timer and tried again.

This time she inhaled so deeply she felt lightheaded. Then she exhaled with such fierceness she felt there couldn't be an iota of air left in her lungs. She returned to a usual breath, taking care to focus on each one.

After some moments, she could not have guessed how many, she heard a timer from somewhere far-off. The sound came across muted, as if blocked by a cliff. She felt as though she were swimming up from some deep place, a place which was both propelling and embracing her. Her limbs felt light and detached, as if they belonged to someone else, and she marveled at their strength and grace.

She was making nothing happen, and yet she could see things *were* happening.

This must be what it feels like to go into labor, she thought. She opened her eyes to see her legs give a slight twitch, then relax, becoming still once more. The timer continued its refrain. She appreciated the expectant sound, and yet she also felt, in some recess of her being, that she wanted to smash it. There were things to do, but she couldn't remember any of them. It was as if her mind had been emptied of memory, her face of expression, her self of personality. If someone had called her name, she wouldn't have known to answer. It was easy to believe that the rug she sat on and the couch she leaned against, as well as the bird tweeting outside, did not exist.

She had gotten "there" but did not know where "there" was. She seemed to float above the notes of the timer. Then finally, all went silent.

Slowly, she moved her fingers and toes, as she had so often told others to do at the end of savasana. She was obedient to the process, and yet there persisted a sensation pulling at her, beckoning her down, down, down into the soft, welcoming waters of meditation. Helpless against it, her eyes closed, and she became once again a citizen in the land where breath rose and fell without effort, bones felt light as air, and muscle was infused with warmth and space. If she could have used words, she might have called it paradise, but there were no words to describe the sensation she felt.

And then, from far off, from somewhere beyond cliff or indeed, from somewhere beyond anything she could identify, there came a crash.

She tried to reclaim any part of self so she could label the noise. At first, it was the sound of a far-off cannon, then after the second crash, it became a tree falling. But when neither seemed right, she opened her eyes, a real effort against heavy lids. Bringing a deep breath down into her relaxed belly, she felt energy return, and when she heard the third crash, she knew something demanded she respond.

In the next moment and in quick succession came a fourth crash and behind it, a fifth, then a sixth. Eugenie, now wholly aware, sprung to her feet and grabbed a broom from the closet. It was a ridiculous move, and even as she did it, she shook her head at the impulse. Then, holding her breath, she listened hard.

The noise was coming from the direction of Arabelle's room. At the door, Eugenie paused for a few seconds, and hearing only a soft whirring sound, she slowly turned the knob.

Having never been inside the room, at least not since it became Arabelle's, Eugenie was surprised to see that little had changed. No personal items were on the desk or side table, or chest of drawers. Pictures on the walls were the ones Eugenie had hung. The bed, however, was now made to hotel standards, sheets taut. The floorboards were dust-free, almost shiny.

For a second, Eugenie exhaled with relief, and that's when the thing came right toward her. Startled, she slammed the broom down for protection.

But the thing was faster, and it hit her foot. One of those robot vacuum cleaners, if she had to guess. She had read about them but had never seen one and, to be sure, had not purchased this one. As it whirred impotently against her foot, she tried to brush it away with the broom. Finally, it changed directions, scooting under the bed and crashing against the wall. In the next moment, as abruptly as it started, it stopped. Chuckling to herself, Eugenie began to shut the door, but stopped when she noticed some trash in the small bin by the desk. She thought of the quiche Arabelle had left for her and decided even though it tasted awful, the least Eugenie could do was empty the bin.

She tucked the two pieces of crumpled paper into the hand which held the broom, and with the other, she closed the door. She put the broom back in the closet, and as she did, the papers fell onto the floor. Leaning over, she picked them up and was ready to throw them into the kitchen trash can, but some vague notion stopped her, and she flattened the papers out on the table for inspection.

She looked down to see photos of a man shot from different angles. They were so blurry as to be practically useless, and she almost crumpled them back up, but again something stopped her. A closer look showed someone she had seen. She was sure of it, but where? She took a seat at the table, brought one image close to her face, and squinted. The man, who was he? She racked her brain, but nothing came up.

And then, leaning back, she remembered.

It wasn't the man she had seen; it was the photo. This was the same photo the security guard had showed her and Ralph when they were sitting in his car at the studio.

# 20

**THE NEXT DAY** had not gone well, and the matter of the photo was banished to the back burner. From the start, Eugenie had characterized the day as "bad," and by doing so, she knew she had made an error in judgment. In yoga philosophy, all days unravel as they are supposed to, and from each so-called "misstep," yogis are to learn from their reaction to the unfolding events. Several times during the day, Eugenie had wanted to grab the philosophers who had written such notions around the throat.

Instead, at the studio, she listened patiently to a litany of complaints from a student fresh out of class.

"The room was too hot," the woman said, bringing her flushed face even closer to Eugenie's as if to submit evidence.

"We set the thermostat to 74 during each class," Eugenie replied.

"Show me. I can't believe it was 74. 84 maybe."

"I'm sorry the room felt uncomfortable to you," said Eugenie. "There are fans attached high on the walls. But the pulls are within reach. Any student is welcome to turn them on."

"And the chatter before class!" said the woman. "I didn't think there was supposed to be talking. Isn't there a sign somewhere to that effect? If I had wanted to hear about that girl's struggle getting her kid to use the toilet, I would have gone to a pediatrician's waiting room."

"You are right about...," Eugenie began.

"And the website! Isn't the covering information supposed to be updated? If I had known you were going...," the woman exclaimed, then stopped.

"To be teaching the class?" Eugenie offered.

The woman's face grew even more red. "Well, yes. We all have our favorites."

Eugenie took in a deep breath and wondered, what in the world would this woman be like if she didn't do yoga?

"I'm sorry things didn't go today as you had hoped," said Eugenie. "The desk can give you a free class to make up for the inconvenience. Tell them what you've told me."

"As if I had the time," the woman replied, pivoting to show Eugenie the back of her expensive multi-strapped mesh top.

Shaking her head, Eugenie found the one cushioned chair in the studio and sunk into it. It had taken a few minutes to find it because, for some reason, this chair was moved from place to place. She relaxed into its pillow-soft back and seat and closed her eyes.

But not for long. "Eugenie," a voice said from above, mispronouncing her name.

Eugenie reluctantly opened her eyelids. "Hmm?" It was the new person from the desk, the one who had replaced Tweedle Dum and Tweedle Dee. Was her name Barbara?

"We double-checked your payroll breakdown like you asked, and what we paid was accurate."

Eugenie tried to sit up in the chair, but with all the padding, it was impossible. Clumsily, she slid back down but managed to get out the words, "The count of the class was off, two students short as I remember."

"It was some time ago," said the person from the desk. "Maybe you got the count wrong?"

"I try to record it in my phone calendar, so I don't think so," said Eugenie.

"I could show you who signed in if that would help. But you probably check that list after class as it is."

Eugenie tried to think back. She didn't always check the sign-in list; had she that day? She couldn't remember.

"No, it's okay. I'll go with what the list shows," Eugenie sighed, for what else was there to say at this point?

Barbara, if that was her name, pointed to the table where a half-full plastic container with the words "Animal Rescue Donations" stood next to the studio suggestion box and said to Eugenie, "Look at how much already and Martha only put this out yesterday. You know how she loves animals, especially dogs. That was the first thing I learned about Martha. But her dog's name, well, that I already forgot." The woman raised her eyebrows in the direction of Eugenie, and finished with, "Anyone can contribute."

Eugenie returned a look that communicated precisely nothing, and the woman left.

Crossing her arms, Eugenie closed her eyes again. She would think about contributing when and only when she was paid by the studio what she was due.

## 21

**THE NEXT DAY** brought a slew of new students to the studio. Why that happened was never clear to Eugenie. Did an article touting the benefits of yoga trend online? Did something shift in the universe that caused people to decide yoga was the way out of their misery? Did a full-length mirror proclaim, "Yoga, you idiot, it's time!"

As it turned out, none of these. Martha had run a social media campaign advertising a significant discount if the newcomer purchased a series of classes in advance. At the front desk, Ralph could be seen amid the crush trying hard to keep his head down.

Eugenie skirted the group, bypassed Barbara, and stood next to Ralph. He didn't look up. Eugenie shuffled her feet, and his eyes still didn't leave the computer. "Ralph," she said in a quiet tone.

"I'm sorry," he said, gaze still frozen on the screen. "Do you think you could... Oh, Eugenie, it's you."

"Real quick, Ralph. I see you're busy. There was a complaint yesterday. From a client. The website isn't updated with the sub's name when the usual teacher is out. Apparently, the client might have thought twice about taking one of my classes if she knew ahead of time."

Ralph scratched at the stubble on his chin. "Nice, real nice. Yeah, I heard. Probably the same person who left a note in the suggestion box, in all caps, if you can believe it. We've got some people subbing today. I'm inputting their names as we speak."

"I won't keep you then," said Eugenie.

"Yeah, better not," he said, eyes focused again on the screen.

Eugenie turned to find Martha standing there, blocking any exit she might have envisioned.

"A word, now, if you please," said Martha.

Ralph swung around, put a hand on Eugenie's shoulder, and said, "She knows, Martha. No need to beat a dead horse."

Eugenie felt her cheeks color as she squirmed within the small space to get out from under the arm, which now rested the length of her shoulder.

"He's right," Eugenie said, "The complaint, I know about it."

"Then you also know the person in question is an influential client," Martha said.

"Thin and rich, that's the way we like them here," Ralph added. At this, Eugenie sucked in her abdomen.

"Keep your voice down," Martha admonished. "When it's your name on the front door, you can have an opinion."

Eugenie continued to squirm, trying to escape Ralph's touch, which had now advanced to a shoulder rub. Nandy, not wanting to be left out, trotted up to the threesome and began licking Eugenie's toes.

Martha took in the picture in front of her. With a movement only a notch less than violent, she scooped up Nandy. For a few seconds, she stared at Ralph and Eugenie. Then slowly, she said, "I was having trouble deciding which day to close the studio for a top-to-bottom clean. I've decided it will be a week from Friday. Ralph, can you put the notice on the website."

It was not a question and Ralph released his arm from Eugenie's shoulder. "Yes, ma'am. Friday. Studio closed for cleaning."

No surprise there, thought Eugenie, making her way out from behind the desk. Friday was the day her most heavily attended classes were scheduled.

# 22

EUGENIE LEFT THE studio only to return a few hours later when she was called to cover a class. As she approached the front door, she saw Ralph exiting. She smiled, but instead of acknowledging her, he let the door slam, causing Eugenie to hit her nose on the glass.

Irritated, she counted to five, then put her fingers on the handle. A sign tacked in a lopsided fashion, its text in red, made her stop for a second time. Above the stenciled, "Welcome to Martha's Mat - Your Life will Change when You Get on Yours" were the words:

"NOTICE! Temporary Fire watch in effect! What this means: The rear fire exits in this building are blocked and under construction. For your safety, Hobson Special Fire Control District requires fire watch duties performed by approved and identifiable personnel who patrol the building watching for signs of smoke and fire. If a fire occurs in this building, call 911 and immediately exit the building by using this door that you entered the building through. DO NOT use any other exits in this building."

At the desk, Eugenie asked Barbara what was going on.

"Oh, you must have come from the other way," said Barbara. "Otherwise, you would have seen the ribbon."

"Ribbon? Eugenie said.

"Miles of yellow ribbon, not really, but a lot," said Barbara. "Strung around the whole strip mall. All the businesses have been told to use only the front doors."

"And this is because...?" said Eugenie.

"That day, remember the one the fire alarm went off," said Barbara. "I wasn't here, but I heard about it. Apparently, a firefighter found everyone out back."

"I remember," said Eugenie. "Go on."

"Well, that day was the day the department inspected the back exits and found most of them, including the studio's, were hazardous, you know, not up to code. The issue is not enough room, not enough cleared space. Anyhow that's how it was explained to me," said Barbara.

"What's the plan then?" said Eugenie.

"Assessment to be collected from each business and work will start," said Barbara.

"Martha knows?" said Eugenie.

"You could say that," said Barbara. "I was coming in when she got off the phone with the fire department. Words came out of her mouth weren't in Sanskrit, I can tell you."

"Anything else I should know?" said Eugenie.

"The thermostat," said Barbara. "Don't touch it. There's a sign. Another sign! Everything's been automatically programmed."

"And if clients complain it's too hot?" said Eugenie.

"DON'T touch it, that's what I've been told," said Barbara.

"Give it a week, the suggestion box will be full," said Eugenie.

"Not the positive thinking I would expect from a yoga instructor," Barbara said, and laughed. "Me, I give it two days. Hot yoga, this studio ain't."

# 23

"**YOU'VE GOT A** drunk student in class." It was the next day and Barbara, looking like she had not slept, still manned the desk.

"What do you mean?" Eugenie asked. "It's not even 10 in the morning."

"Nevertheless, she's drunk. Smelled it on her breath when she arrived. There," Barbara pointed to a scribble on the sign-in sheet. "That's the one."

"I don't recognize the name," said Eugenie. "Does Martha know?'

"She's gone, somewhere, not sure where," said Barbara.

"Did you talk to the client?" said Eugenie. "Try to convince her to not take the class?"

"Above my pay grade," said Barbara. "Good luck. It's not safe, her wobbling around like that."

"Tell me about it. Great, just great," Eugenie said, turning to go into class. She had not traveled two feet when the smell of alcohol reached her. "Vicky?" she called out.

A man coming out of the props room blocked her from going further. "You the teacher?" he asked.

"Hi, yes, I'm Eugenie. You're?"

"Oliver. Lady at the desk said you might ask if there are any health issues or injuries you should know about. Reason being, you don't want to make things worse, is my guess. No injuries, but I will divulge my doctor says I have high blood pressure."

Eugenie looked him over and was not surprised. He was overweight and his face was the color of ripe tomato. "Is it controlled? Are you on medication?" she asked.

"I won't take pills," Oliver announced. "Don't believe in them. That's why I'm here. "

"I see," said Eugenie. "You're thinking yoga will lower your blood pressure?"

"Don't you?" he asked.

"Might," said Eugenie, "Might not."

Out of the corner of her eye, Eugenie saw Barbara at the desk waving a liability release form and mouthing, "Signed."

Eugenie sighed and looked back at the man. "All right, take it easy. That's my best advice. Go slow and take it easy. Now," Eugenie said, facing the rest of the class, "Is Vicky here?"

"Accounted and present for," came a voice from the back of the room. Eugenie followed the scent.

To appear casual and not have the rest of the class hear, Eugenie stood close to the woman, balanced on one foot, swinging the other behind her. The move was not successful, and she fell into Vicky, who, thinking this was the funniest thing she'd seen all day, burst into laughter and remarked, "Jared said you might be like this."

Eugenie's ears perked up at the name. "Like what?"

"Funny, hysterically funny," said Vicky.

Eugenie, who had never felt less funny in her life, whispered, "Are you drunk? It's not safe to take the class if you are."

"Jared said it's not safe to take the class if you aren't." More laughter. Eugenie looked at the woman, who crossed her arms and stared back. They were at a standstill. In the next moment it was broken by an unlikely source.

Oliver, all two hundred and fifty pounds of him, approached. He said nothing, merely gathered up Vicky's mat after tugging twice to make sure she got off it, rolled it up, and handed it to her.

Then to her astonished expression, he spoke the words, "Like I've always said, Miss. Clean is best."

Vicky hugged the mat like it was a shield and headed to the door, but not before spitting out a threat the entire class could hear: "My landscaper will be in touch."

"I think she meant lawyer," said Oliver to no one in particular, "But to make sure, everyone keep their lawn mowed."

# 24

**"GREAT, SO SHE'S** going to sue," said Martha.

"She's not going to sue," said Eugenie.

They were in Martha's office, a cramped space tucked next to the front desk. Eugenie stood between a stacked washer and dryer and a collection of fake Native American blankets, plump bolsters, and shiny patterned silk pillows. A window, large enough to let in a blast of sunlight at that hour, was partially obscured by a line of essential oil bottles, two without caps. The fragrance emitted was unpleasant, proving that once again, tea tree and eucalyptus do not go well together.

Against her better judgment, Eugenie took in a deep breath. "I thought you should know what happened, that's all."

Looking out the window, Martha stayed silent. Her hands were clenched, fingernails leaving an arc of indentation in her waistband. "My car needs washing," she finally said, pointing out the window. "You see?" she asked. The question must have been rhetorical because, in the small room, there was no way Eugenie could maneuver to get the same view.

Martha didn't wait for an answer and said, "Because of the birds, I never park under a tree. Today, the space was taken, and look, droppings all over the hood. And it's not even noon."

Eugenie nodded sympathetically. "So, we're done?"

"No," said Martha, pirouetting to face Eugenie, "We are not done. She says she was embarrassed by the teacher."

"Who?" said Eugenie.

"The client," Martha said, close to stamping her foot. "Vicky!"

"I don't see how she could have been," said Eugenie. "I tried to keep the conversation private. You know, whispering it wasn't safe in the state she was in. She was the one with the loud voice. Ask Oliver. He was there."

"For heaven's sake," said Martha. "I'm not going to ask Oliver, whoever Oliver is."

"He was one of the...," began Eugenie.

"Never mind," said Martha. "I'm not going to make this thing worse by questioning every Dick and Harry. Nobody understands what it's like being an owner. The things you think about. The things you worry about."

"She won't sue, really," said Eugenie. "It wasn't that big a deal."

"To you maybe. You're only the teacher. So, she won't take your class again, big whoop. My studio and name she'll blacken all over the Internet."

Eugenie leaned back against the dryer and the door, which had been left ajar, slammed shut. She reacted to the sound by moving to the side, and the tower of pillows fell over. "Oops," said Eugenie, picking them up.

"Never mind," said Martha, throwing up her hands. "Leave them, leave them. It's been that kind of day. Nobody understands, that's all."

Eugenie moved over to stand at the door that was propped open by a small Buddha statue. "We all try, Martha, we really do. Perhaps a yoga class would help?"

Martha looked at Eugenie like she had lost her mind. "Beyond the boatload I teach every week, you mean?"

"No, I mean, take one. For a change," said Eugenie, her voice coming out little more than a squeak. "That way, no pressure. Relax, beginner's mind, and all that."

It wasn't clear if Martha had heard or not, but as she started throwing blankets into the washing machine, there was no mistaking the conversation was at an end. "These are not going to clean themselves," she said, shaking her head. "That's what nobody understands."

_25_

**IN THE PARKING** lot, Eugenie was dismayed to find it was her car in "Martha's space," not that there was any way to tell it was assigned as such. But just in case Martha was watching from the office window, Eugenie headed in another direction across the lot. The last thing she needed was to have Martha hold a parking space against her. While concentrating on how that conversation might play out, she almost tripped over a cord laying on the pavement. She reached down to untangle her foot and Nandy, attached to the other end, careened toward her, all four paws scraping along the pavement.

"What the…!" said Eugenie, picking up the small creature and looking around to see who or what was attached to the other end of the extendable lead.

"Fritzi's the name," said a loud voice.

"No, pretty sure it's Nandy. The dog's name is Nandy," said Eugenie.

"No, MY name. My name's Fritzi," said a woman coming toward them.

"A car could have hit her," said Eugenie, holding the dog close. "This parking lot can be crazy busy. You should be more careful."

"Hey, don't you tell me my business," said Fritzi. "I was watching. There was no danger. Well, from you, maybe. You really should look where you're going."

"And you are?" asked Eugenie.

"Dog walker Fritzi. Martha hired me to babysit Nandy. Been on the job, for, I don't know, dog years," she said, laughing hard. She pulled a cigarette from a stained hip pouch and offered it to Eugenie.

"Take one," said Fritzi. "Helps with the weight."

"Look, I'm a yoga teacher," said Eugenie. "Wouldn't help with that."

"You are? Shut the fuck up. You sure don't look like one," said Fritzi. "Positive you don't want a smoke?"

By this time Fritzi had taken the dog back and they were sitting on the hood of a pickup truck which, by the looks of it, had never seen better days. Still worried that Martha see her anywhere near her parking space, Eugenie took a seat next to Fritzi. The cigarette which was even now being proffered was accepted, if reluctantly. Fritzi lit it with a little too much relish and watched as Eugenie coughed.

"Didn't know what you were missing," Fritzi said, grinning ear to ear.

The three sat side by side in silence on the hood of the truck, smoke curling up through the branches of the oak tree above them.

After a few moments, Fritzi announced, "I was one, too, you know, a yoga teacher."

Eugenie cast a sideways glance, which Fritzi took as disbelief. "I was, ask anybody."

"So, what happened?" asked Eugenie, nodding toward the dog. "Why this gig?"

"I never got paid, not what I was owed, and I got sick of it, plain sick of asking for payroll breakdowns that I shouldn't have had to ask for. Damn it all, they never got the class count right. Well, maybe once or twice, but really, are you kidding? It frosted me and one day I got tired of it, and I quit."

"So how did you end up...," said Eugenie.

"Dog sitter to Nandy?" said Fritzi. "Martha was desperate. Gal before me had adios'd, gone to New Zealand or Newfoundland, anyways someplace new, with some guy, and well, you know Martha, anything for the dog."

"Weren't you worried you wouldn't get paid for this job either?" said Eugenie.

"Bet I was, but I got smart," said Fritzi. "Everything's in cash. I made that crystal-clear up front." She turned Nandy around and held her so she and the terrier were eye to eye: "Dogs have their uses. No payee, no walkee, right Nandy?"

The dog wiggled out of Fritzi's hands and onto Eugenie's lap.

"Hey, she likes you," Fritzi declared. "A sweet thing, unlike her owner, not that I would want you to go repeating that. Can you believe the woman doesn't tell staff they're eligible for a raise after they've been at the studio for a year? Somehow, she figures they are to know, by osmosis, telepathy, whatever - it's nuts. If you ask me, woman's cheap, cheap as they come."

Having taken all she could of the cigarette and figuring by now it must be safe, Eugenie slid off the hood of the truck. When her feet hit the pavement, her knees buckled and before she knew it, Fritzi was holding her up by the armpits, saving her by inches from hitting the ground.

"Whoa, partner," Fritzi cautioned. "Take it easy. I roll them myself. That way, they're strong. Probably what's giving you sea legs."

But Eugenie knew the cigarette was only part of the problem. The real issue was that no one, and certainly not Martha, had told Eugenie she was eligible for a raise at any time during the years she'd been teaching at the studio.

# 26

**FUELED BY ANGER** more than gasoline, Eugenie drove to a yoga studio, which, according to her phone, was a good fifty minutes away. There, she signed the requisite release of liability form, paid for a single class, and laid her mat toward the back of the room in the shadow of a struggling potted palm. No one knew her, and she knew no one, and for a time the anonymity soothed her. Her diaphragm relaxed and breathing came easier.

And then the teacher began to chant.

A harsher sound had never come out of anyone's mouth. Fingernails on slate would have been an improvement. His "Om" was so discordant Eugenie had to stifle a laugh. She looked around to see if it surprised others, but no one else reacted. They all looked as if this was normal.

Well, it wasn't. It was awful and someone should have told this guy never ever chant. Don't chant, don't sing, don't talk, maybe only whisper. For several minutes, she fought the urge to leave and then, realizing how it would look, she considered covering her ears.

Finally, mercifully, the chanting was over, and the physical portion of the class began. That was when she remembered she had signed up for a Vinyasa class, which meant that once everyone got the hang of the sequence, the teacher would stop talking. Relieved when that happened, Eugenie surrendered to the vigorous dancelike practice, and soon sweat slid down her back. As her breathing stabilized, she fell deeper and deeper into concentration. After savasana was over, the morning's revelation had lost much of its punch, and she gathered up her mat. But before she could get out the door, she found herself face to face with the instructor.

She watched as he offered a large hand to shake, and, accepting it, she apologized.

"For what?" he said. "You did great. I was going to thank you for bringing your energy to class today."

Before she could respond, the skies outside erupted, and the sound of thunder accompanied by a roar of rain penetrated the walls of the studio.

The man paused, looking at Eugenie as if he were deep in thought. After a moment, he said softly, "It appears you have manifested a great storm."

"I'm really sorry," apologized Eugenie for the second time. With that and an awkward bow, she darted out of the studio.

In the car, she whacked her forehead with her palm. He had been kind, and she hadn't been, not at all. He couldn't help the voice he'd been given, but she could help her attitude, and she wondered, once again, why she hadn't.

She turned the key in the ignition with such force it balked. After a few more tries, the car started up. Taking one wrong turn, then another, she finally found the route to the interstate, which, because of the rain, was almost as slow as the side road she'd just left.

Chalk it up to bad karma. Well, she deserved it. The cars inching along gave her time to think. When she reached the outskirts of her hometown, she knew what she would do.

**THE FAST FOOD,** still hot from the drive-through, was placed, almost ceremoniously by Eugenie, on the kitchen table. Her stomach growling in anticipation, she twisted to grab a plate out of the cupboard, then turned to find the bags gone.

"What the...?" she said, looking around.

"I confess," said Arabelle, peeking around the corner of the kitchen. "Mea culpa big time."

"If you were hungry, why didn't you say so?" said Eugenie. "I would have shared."

"Are you kidding?" said Arabelle. "I wouldn't put that stuff in my body, not for all the subpoenas at the justice department."

"Well then, give it back," said Eugenie. "Now."

"No can do. Already in the trash in the garage," said Arabelle.

"Look, I'm hungry and in no mood to quarrel," said Eugenie.

"Check the frig then," said Arabelle.

Eugenie looked incredulous at the idea. "The frig?"

"Yeah, the frig," said Arabelle. "What your spirit really desires. Go. See."

Wanting to do nothing less, Eugenie opened the door to the refrigerator. A riot of color, from deep reds to blazing yellows to vivid greens, met her stare.

Arabelle nodded, pleased with herself. "There's enough to feed an army. I went shopping. Since the quiche disappeared in a heartbeat, I figured you wanted more."

"Oh God," said Eugenie, "You think that I...?"

"Deep down crave that healthy stuff, well yeah," said Arabelle. "The way you downed it."

Eugenie, reluctant to explain what really happened to the quiche, just stood silent.

"Give it a few weeks, and you'll get used to it," said Arabelle. "You'll forget you ever craved a cheeseburger."

Eugenie sighed. "All right then, let's eat. It's not like I'm not hungry."

Arabelle got to work making an enormous salad and fresh dressing. She placed a portion on a plate in front of Eugenie.

Eugenie raised her eyebrows and said, "Well, I'll give you an A for presentation, anyway." After taking a bite, she looked back at Arabelle, expecting her to be making her own salad. When instead she put the rest into a large bowl in the frig, Eugenie said, "You're not joining me?"

"Got to go," Arabelle said, checking her cell. "Duty calls."

"Now?" said Eugenie. "I thought this was your day off."

"What can I say? Things change. On a mission or rather the life of a drudge, take your pick," said Arabelle.

"You can spare a minute," said Eugenie. "To talk about rent. The amount you pay."

Arabelle stepped forward, her lanky frame towering over Eugenie at the kitchen table. "No problem, we can talk, then got to go," she said, pulling a wad of cash out of her jean's pocket. "Forgot my pack. Back in a sec."

Eugenie took a desultory bite of salad, then proceeded to count the wrinkled money. She felt her jaw drop, and a carrot fell out of her mouth. "It's too much!" she said to herself, then yelled so Arabelle could hear.

In a flash, her tenant was back, dressed as if she was going anywhere but an office.

Eugenie glanced up at her. "Look, this covers...," said Eugenie, trying to do the math in her head and failing. "Well, I don't know how many months. Why?"

"Since no telling how long I'm staying, I didn't want you to worry," said Arabelle. "Consider it manna. You know, from heaven."

Not daring to ask what exactly manna was, Eugenie said, "It's a lot of money." Enough to cover rent plus the canceled classes when the studio was closed for cleaning.

"Now, what was it you wanted to talk about?" said Arabelle.

Eugenie laughed, "Nothing, exactly nothing."

"See you when I see you," said Arabelle. And in the next instant, she was out the door, giving Eugenie only a glimpse of the gear slung from her back.

*28*

**THE PHOTO, EUGENIE** thought, as she stabbed repeatedly at the lettuce in the salad. She had meant to ask Arabelle about the photo. Resolving to do so the next time she saw her, Eugenie lifted her fork, which contained more than any one person could put in their mouth at a time. Maybe more than a growing manatee could. All she could think of was that she wanted to get this meal over with.

She tried to appreciate what she was eating but failed. She craved salt. She craved sugar. Then she remembered.

There was a bag of chocolate chip cookies somewhere in the kitchen. She had hidden them from Arabelle, unnecessarily, as it turns out. More to the point, she had hidden them from herself. Where could she have put them?

In the third cabinet she opened, she came across a handheld wooden labyrinth. It fell onto the counter as she moved bowls and pie plates aside and behind it, lo and behold, were the cookies. Before she reached the table, the package was ripped open. Grateful there was no one to see, she stuffed two cookies in her mouth. Unlike the salad, the cookies went down easily. She sighed happily as the sugar hit her tongue.

On the counter, the labyrinth tottered. Eugenie lunged to catch it before it hit the floor, then placed it back on the ledge. It had been a gift from a student, she vaguely recalled, and she had not treated it, she realized now, with much respect. To make up for that, she examined it with interest.

The maze was the size of two hands, and it appeared to be fashioned from a hardwood, maybe teak. In her grasp, the object felt light. She inspected it front and back and discovered the origin was Burma. A labyrinth on the ground was something she knew. She had walked one years ago at a local church, the occasion long since forgotten. Walking a labyrinth was a meditative journey, helping some find stillness, others focus.

She held the miniature labyrinth lightly in her right hand and, following her inclination as a child, she traced the smooth indentations of the maze with her left index finger.

For a time, she concentrated only on the curves of the pattern, and her thoughts drifted to wonder who made them. Then, as her finger rounded the second turn, her thoughts switched to Jared. She tried to resist by bringing her attention back to the finger, which continued to trace the spiral path, slowly and methodically making its way toward the center, and for a time, she was successful.

But when she reached the last groove, the one which led to the midpoint of the maze, the image of his body came to her in sharp relief. She felt her breath quicken as, in her mind's eye, she traced the scar near his left shoulder, then a second scar above his knee, and the last one the length of his shinbone. After circling the small pinecone tattoo above his ankle, she traveled up the one unscathed leg, and there she saw her finger pause, nesting in the thatch of hair at the base of his erection.

The desire she felt the times they were together washed over her, and close behind it, the all too familiar shame. She stuffed two more cookies in her mouth and tossed the labyrinth back in the cupboard.

## 29

IT WAS NOT yet dawn when Eugenie entered the studio lot a few days later. She parked the car, taking care to guide it into a space under a tree, one Martha would never think to claim. Opening the door, she stopped. She could see a dark figure moving purposefully from one car to the next, pausing at each to peer underneath. Her hand tight on the door handle, she tried to make out who the figure was. The parking lot lights were no help. Two out of the four were lit, and even those flickered. It was only when a light was switched on by someone inside the studio that she could see.

It was Ralph.

"What the hell?" she said when she caught up to him.

"Oh Eugenie, it's you," he said, looking relieved. "Martha's on the warpath."

"I'm going to need more," said Eugenie. "What are you doing?"

"You know the feather flag?" said Ralph.

Eugenie returned a blank look.

"You must. The feather flag!" said Ralph. "It's, I don't know, six feet tall, a purple thing that says 'Yoga' on it in big letters."

"Oh, the feather flag, didn't know that's what it was called," said Eugenie. "Yes, I've seen it, usually planted on the green strip near where the traffic on the main road passes."

"That's the one," said Ralph. "Well, it's gone. Martha thinks someone took it. Well, being Martha, she would. Me, I think the wind might have carried it into the parking lot, maybe under a car. Some of the business owners come in early, so I'm checking under theirs. Here, take the flashlight and help."

"My class starts soon," said Eugenie.

"For the sake of peace and harmony in the studio," said Ralph, "You can give me five."

Eugenie sighed, took the flashlight, and headed toward the furthest car. Feeling silly, she stooped, directing the light under the car. No flag. She trotted over to the next car and shone the flashlight. Again, nothing. The last car was more than a few steps away, and this time, irritated at what she regarded as a fool's errand, she let herself plod. At the rear tire, she squatted, thinking, if nothing else, this was a good warm-up for her Achilles' tendons. She directed the stream of light under the car, placed one hand on the pavement, and bent over so she could see.

As she did, she came face to face with not a flag, but an eye. She blinked, forcing the light in her hand to remain steady, not sure what she was seeing.

Unblinking, the eye stared back at her. Slowly, she moved the flashlight to the left, and when scales appeared, one row after another, she jumped up and ran as fast as she could toward Ralph.

"Hey!" he yelled, almost toppling over at the force with which she hit him.

"There's a...," Eugenie blurted, pointing.

They watched as the startled creature, a good nine feet long, took off at a sprinter's pace across the parking lot and over to the side of the studio. From the plants which hugged the side and back of the building came a crashing sound as branches were trampled and broke.

In the ensuing silence, Ralph continued to hold the shaken Eugenie. They stood frozen under the parking lot lights which, assisted by the rising sun, gave Martha, standing at the door of the studio, a clear picture of the scene unfolding before her.

**30**

**"TELL NO ONE,"** Martha declared after she had recovered from the sight of seeing Eugenie in Ralph's arms.

"About the...," began Ralph.

"Alligator?" finished Eugenie.

"You don't know that for sure," said Martha. "It makes no sense to talk about something when we don't know what it was."

Ralph and Eugenie looked as if someone had punched the air out of them. For a moment, no one said anything.

Finally, Martha spoke up, "I take it you didn't find the flag. Stolen's my guess, and those things aren't cheap."

At this, Ralph recovered his voice. "Forget the damn flag, Martha. We are talking about an alligator. Under someone's car. In this parking lot. Its jaws inches from one of the studio's teachers. And we're not going to tell anyone?"

"No, we're not," Martha replied.

"But Martha," Eugenie said. "The damage it could do. Kill even."

"If that's what it was, which we don't know," said Martha.

Ralph had lost his patience. "What the hell else is that long and can fit under a car? And runs like it ran."

"With slit eyes. I saw them," said Eugenie, raising the flashlight still clutched in her hand.

"Listen, you two," Martha said, waving her arm. "This is my studio, and alligators aren't good for business. There was no alligator." Over her shoulder, she added, "Don't you have work to do? I suggest you get to it."

Eugenie tried to hand the flashlight to Ralph, who ignored it, saying something under his breath that in the quiet of the studio, sounded a lot like "bitch."

_31_

**"YOU LOOK PALE,"** one of the students said as Eugenie entered the class. "You really do," said another, pulling a chair over for her to sit down. Eugenie obeyed and a student reached for the flashlight in her hands, saying, "Unless there's a blackout, I don't think you're going to be needing this." Gently, the woman took the light and asked, "Want to tell us what's going on?"

"Tough morning," said Eugenie, taking in their concerned faces, grateful that Jared no longer took this class. "Need a minute, if it's okay with you."

"Sure," said Callie. "You're always there for us. Time we took care of you. What say we do a little alternate nostril breathing?"

"That might help," said Eugenie, and Callie, taking over, directed the class to start.

It was a breathing exercise familiar to this group, and they responded by putting their right thumbs to their right nostrils and inhaling through the left nostril. Then, closing the left nostril with the little finger, they exhaled through the right. This continued until Eugenie felt herself shift into teacher mode and said, "Better, thanks."

"Alternate nostril unites the right and left sides of the brain, the reasoning and the creative," said Eugenie. "It brings balance. Did you feel it?"

"More importantly," said Callie from the front row of chairs. "Did you?"

"Yes, think so," said Eugenie, and she began to demonstrate the first asana, a pose bringing the gaze of the eyes to the armpit as the palm of the hand rested on the back of the head.

She told herself she was okay and for a while during the neck and shoulder stretches, she was. But as the class progressed, unease took over. A few times, she repeated asanas on the same side. Then, she cued a pose so vaguely the class struggled to follow. By the time she introduced the side stretches with one hand resting on the floor and the other elevated, she lost her balance momentarily, almost falling off the chair and ending up on the floor.

At last, the clock on the wall announced the time for savasana. She invited the class to relax, to let the chair underneath take all their weight as they sat upright, feet flat on the floor. Because of the late start to the class, it was a short meditation and when finished, she was relieved to wish them all a good day.

Only Callie lingered at the door. "You okay?" she asked.

"Sure," said Eugenie. "Everything's fine. Nothing like yoga to set things right."

"If you say so," Callie said, the concern not leaving her face. "When you were cueing us to get into warrior pose..."

"Oh, too complicated?" said Eugenie. "On a chair is different from the mat."

"No, that wasn't it," said Callie. "When you introduced warrior pose, instead of calling it warrior..."

"What?" said Eugenie.

Callie said, "You called it worrier."

# 32

**TWO DAYS LATER,** Martha called a mandatory meeting of the studio staff. The appointed time was not an issue for Eugenie, but she could tell by social media posts it was a big deal for some of her fellow teachers as they scrambled to get coverage for classes they taught at other studios.

"What's up, do you think?" asked Sarah that night as she got out of her car and jogged over to Eugenie's.

"Search me," said Eugenie, wondering if Martha had changed her mind about the alligator.

"If it's about that guy in the photo," said Sarah, "I'm going to scream. If I've told the security guard once, I've told her fifty times. I don't know who he is. And if it's about Jared, I'm over the guy. You too, if you're lucky."

Eugenie stopped and faced Sarah. "You know about that?"

"Anybody with ears knows about that," said Sarah. "He has one big mouth."

Eugenie looked down, her hands pressed to her waist. "Unbelievable."

Sarah followed her gaze. "You're not pregnant by any chance?"

"No!" said Eugenie, her voice so loud a man going into the title office next to the studio turned in alarm.

"In what we wear," said Sarah, "An extra pound or two is noticeable, that's all."

"Well, I'm not," said Eugenie. "The weight is the result, if you must know, of stuff I shouldn't be eating."

"Well, good for you, that you're not," said Sarah. "Those of us who've been thrown off the Jared train, we got to stick together."

And here, Sarah wasn't kidding. When they got inside, she put her mat so close to Eugenie's that if they had been doing poses, their arms would have whacked the other's chin.

When all the teachers and desk staff had arrived, Martha made what could only be called an entrance. Her body would have been a source of pride for a twenty-year-old; for a woman over fifty, it was a miracle of nature. Eugenie watched as Martha tugged at a top that didn't need adjusting, a gesture that could only be interpreted as bringing attention to chiseled abdominal muscles.

"Hey," Sarah whispered to Eugenie. "I thought we were never to wear those. No midriffs showing, isn't that the rule?"

Up front, Martha cleared her throat. "If I could have everyone's attention." From the parking lot, the sound of a car made it difficult to hear, and Eugenie leaned forward.

Martha continued, "We have a lot to cover, and I want to get started. There are snacks for everyone after the meeting. Help yourself at the front desk."

"Fuck," whispered Sarah. "Snacks. That's code for we're not getting paid to attend this bullshit thing."

"You have a question?" asked Martha, and not waiting for an answer, she said, "No? Good."

In the front of the classroom, a large mirror reflected Fritzi and Nandy on the other side of the plate-glass window behind the teachers. Fritzi was taking the dog through her paces, going back and forth, back and forth. Eugenie watched as a gentle breeze rustled Fritzi's unkempt mane and Nandy's carefully groomed coat.

In the distance, the noise from the offending car continued, giving Martha no choice but to stop talking and wait for it to cease. On the sidewalk, Nandy hesitated by a trash receptacle to concentrate on what looked like a candy wrapper curled in a wad on the ground. Before the dog could bring it to her mouth, Fritzi scooped the dog up. As she cuddled the terrier in her arms, she said something to Nandy which made the dog lurch forward, tongue extended to lick every inch of the dog walker's freckled face. Fritzi burst into giggles.

Eugenie turned from the sight, closed her eyes, and wished, for a moment, she was a dog.

## 33

**WHEN THE NOISE** from the parking lot finally stopped, Martha said, "Eyes front, this is serious, people."

In the corner of the room, Ralph sighed and picked at something on his jeans. He raised his eyes just long enough for Eugenie to see them roll. Beside him, Sarah gazed with satisfaction at her reflection in the mirror. On the other side of the room was Barbara, looking, by the pained expression on her face, as if she had not sat on the floor since she left kindergarten. Only Eugenie's eyes were on Martha. She wondered if this was a good time to bring up a raise.

"I'm passing out...," the studio owner began.

"Give her air, give her air," whispered Sarah to Eugenie, who brought her finger to her lips and said, "Old joke."

"... some reminders for the clients and teachers," finished Martha, glaring at Sarah. "I'll give you a moment to look over."

Eugenie skimmed the list, which included everything from punching in without having to be reminded to paying attention to personal hygiene. In total, there were twenty-five items. Martha was in full micro-manager mode.

To the group, the studio owner said, "I ask that you bring your attention to item number five. You," Martha said, pointing at Sarah, "Will you read aloud?"

Sarah straightened and whispered to Eugenie, "Nothing like being back in third grade." Then clearing her throat, she read, "Number five: Remind your students about workshops and how they can sign up." After a pause, she looked at Martha and said, "But I do. I have."

"At the beginning of every class?" said Martha.

"No," allowed Sarah. "But at least once I have."

"What do I have to do to get through to you people? Before every single class, workshops are to be mentioned," Martha said.

Eugenie leaned back against the window. Of course. Workshops were where Martha made most of her money. And as Eugenie held no workshops, where Eugenie would make none. This being an independent contractor was sometimes for the birds. The teachers were expected to support the entire work of the studio, but they were paid only for the classes they taught. Plus, what teachers were paid was a pittance of what the client paid, the rest going for studio expenses or into Martha's pocket.

Martha had her teachers over a barrel, and she knew it. And the thing was, the teachers knew it too. If they complained, there was always someone eager to take their place. Not necessarily someone good, but someone.

Martha broke into Eugenie's thoughts: "You look like you have something on your mind. Share, why don't you?"

Eugenie squirmed, thought for a moment about letting it all rip, then sunk back against the window, and said, "Tax returns take more time when you're an independent contractor. No W-2s, which make it so much easier to file."

All eyes were now on Eugenie, with those teachers who hadn't worked at the studio long enough to file a return, looking worried.

"That's what you were thinking?" said Martha. "My fault for having asked."

Instead of requesting any of the other teachers read, Martha read the rest of the list herself and without enthusiasm. It was as if Eugenie had launched a trial balloon, and whatever Martha said after that held little interest. She was not a dim person, and recognizing the dynamics, Martha concluded with, "There's a copy on the front desk for each of you, next to the snacks."

In a flash, the room emptied to gather around the front desk, and even though most of the staff except Eugenie looked as if they had eaten little more than kale in the past week, they dove into the food. Between bites, there was the usual chatter about exercise bras and non-staining deodorants, super-absorbent tampons, discounts on yoga gear, and rumors about jobs at gyms that might pay more. Topics could change on a dime and did when Martha drew near. Eugenie listened with half an ear, saving the bulk of her attention for some bear claw pastry, grateful but astounded that it had somehow made its way to a place between the dried prunes and the vegan chips and even more grateful that her position tucked against the wall shielded her from disapproving glances.

After a while, the group, sated by calories and talk, quieted, and it was clear everyone was getting ready to leave.

It was then Fritzi, hair even wilder than usual, bolted from the back of the studio and rushed up to Martha. Eugenie watched as the dog walker tried to speak. At first, nothing came out but a spray of saliva. Martha, in the process of lifting a celery stick to her lips, stepped back in distaste and said, "What the...?"

"She's gone!" Fritzi finally blurted out.

"Who's gone?" said Martha.

"Nandy!" said Fritzi.

"That's ridiculous," said Martha. "Of course she isn't."

"I've searched everywhere," said Fritzi, and as if that wasn't enough to get the room's attention, she repeated the "everywhere" several times. "Dog's nowhere to be found."

Martha put her hand on a plate of food as if to hold herself up. It toppled to the floor where a single stuffed mushroom escaped and began to roll. Transfixed, everyone stopped and watched in silence as the finger food made the journey down the hallway to the back wall of the studio.

And there it hit with a small thud.

Eugenie would remember this as the last peaceful moment any of them would know.

# 34

**STILL TUCKED IN** the corner, Eugenie watched as frenzy erupted. Yoga teachers, their bodies supple and firm, stretched high and low, looking for the dog. Someone turned on music, and a pounding beat, definitely not the usual fourth-world music, bounced off every surface. The bass, the only thing identifiable over the din of the search, sounded like 80s disco, and Eugenie wondered if that was the music imprinted from the studio owner's youth.

Eugenie listened and took another bite of the bear claw.

To say the pastry tasted good was an understatement. After the Arabelle days of romaine and cucumber, the sugar hit Eugenie's tongue like cocaine. It took everything in her not to turn giddy.

Sarah poked her head into view and swatted at Eugenie's thigh. "She better not find you doing zip." And then, "I wasn't paying attention. What is the name and breed of the dog we're looking for?"

Sarah's question was ridiculous. It was a dog. If they found a dog in the studio, that was probably the dog that was missing. Eugenie hesitated, then began, "It's a terrier named..."

But too late. Sarah had been grabbed by another teacher who wanted help emptying the props room.

Better her than me, thought Eugenie, thinking of musty bolsters and endless foam blocks piled to the ceiling.

The studio, never huge, began to feel claustrophobic. Exertion from the teachers caused every window to fog. Eugenie looked at the glass closest to her and was tempted to draw a smiley face. Then, seeing a last bear claw, she reached for it.

The pastry was almost to her mouth when the music stopped abruptly, leaving only the sound of chanting. Martha's voice, a pitch higher than usual but still recognizable, repeated something in Sanskrit—a mantra Eugenie recognized. Well, Martha knew a million of them.

A week ago, after an encounter with a student who demanded her money back, Martha could be heard chanting non-stop. That had irritated Eugenie because, in the next room, she'd been trying to teach. The chant also didn't seem like it worked because afterward, Martha made a point of lighting several sage smudge sticks, which might have cleared the negative vibe left by the student, but did nothing for the throats of those who coughed and hacked as they exited Eugenie's classroom. In Eugenie's opinion, Martha's ideas sometimes made things worse.

Curious about what would happen next, Eugenie took a bite out of the bear claw and simultaneously pulled in her stomach. She was momentarily cheered by the fact the weight wouldn't show until the next day.

It wasn't until she felt something pressing against her leg that Eugenie jumped off the counter. In the next instant, she fell into Fritzi, who was occupied tilting a water cooler.

"You really think Nandy could squeeze behind that?" Eugenie said.

Fritzi craned her neck to look at Eugenie. This unfortunate move caused the full water bottle to slip out of the stand and empty all over the floor.

"I'll get something!" said Eugenie.

"Doesn't matter," said Fritzi, looking at the flood. "Nandy's gone. My job too."

Eugenie, hands now full of paper towels, tried to think of something comforting to say.

"It's not over until the fat lady sings," was all she could come up with.

## 35

**DESPITE EXPERIENCING THE** occasional premonition, it was not something Eugenie relied on. In fact, it was not something she even remembered about herself. That is, until the next time it happened.

Yesterday.

When Fritzi rushed in to say the dog was gone, Eugenie knew in every fiber of her being that the dog really was gone. Gone from the studio.

Not dead, however. How she knew this, she couldn't say, but from time to time, some force informed her of things she couldn't know in the usual ways. Like the time when her clueless father was about to embarrass her publicly. Like the time she knew she was going to miscarry, again. Like the time she knew to hesitate even when a light had turned green, only missing by inches being hit by a soused teenager.

She pinched the flesh around her waist. "Hello bear claw!" But saying so didn't have the usual effect and in this, she was surprised.

For once, there was something to think about besides her weight.

There was Nandy.

She picked up her phone and typed in the browser, "How to find lost dog."

First on the list was to search the immediate surroundings. Done, she thought, remembering the chaos in the studio. Next on the list was...

A text popped up. It was from Martha and said, "Help required. Wear usual clothes."

What could that mean? Wear usual clothes? Did that mean wear clothes as usual? No, that didn't seem right. What clothes were usual clothes? It was hot outside. Did that mean shorts and a sleeveless top?

Eugenie looked to see who the text was addressed to. A long list of names. She recognized it as the studio's teacher roster. Usual clothes must mean yoga clothes. Those were the only clothes Martha typically saw them in.

Eugenie ran to her bedroom and threw off her nightie. It landed on the floor next to the clothes she was wearing the night before. She picked the top up, and a large crumb fell out. Recognizing it as from a bear claw, she popped it in her mouth. Mmm, stale, but still good. She searched for the dirty clothes basket and found it half filled with trash, which she emptied on the floor. From beneath the pile emerged something that crawled.

"Palmetto!" she cried, even though anyone else would have said, "Roach."

From a nightstand, she found an empty cup and some cardboard. She lunged at the speedy creature, covering it at the last moment before it scurried under the bed. She slid the cardboard under the cup. Balancing both, she made her way to the back door, which she kicked open with one foot. Then she uncovered the cup and shook it hard. Instead of flying out toward the backyard, the bug dropped next to her slipper, where she, with some regret, promptly stomped on it.

"Well," said Eugenie. "I tried."

Putting the roach into the trash, she glimpsed at herself in a mirror. Naked as the day she'd been cut from her mother's body.

Thank goodness Arabelle was not around. A naked landlady. That was a lot to ask of any renter, much less the elusive Arabelle.

Against all odds, maybe there was something clean to wear. Eugenie checked drawers one after another until, with little hope, she got to her sock drawer. And there, amazingly, was a clean pair of tights and a yoga top. Next to them was the crumpled photo she had found in Arabelle's room.

She picked up the photo and stared hard at the face. Still nothing. Already, the day hadn't made much sense, and it was just beginning.

# 36

**EUGENIE WAS BARELY** out of the car when Sarah was upon her. Dressed in a halter top and the shortest of shorts, she gave Eugenie a look that could only be described as confused.

"I thought usual clothes meant what you normally wear," said Sarah.

"I thought, oh never mind," said Eugenie. "What've you got there?"

Sarah thumbed through a stack of papers and passed half over to Eugenie. From her waistband, she pulled out a stapler and a roll of tape. "See those posts?" Sarah said, pointing toward the road. "Martha wants these on every one."

Eugenie looked at a flyer. The word "missing" took up most of the page, followed by a photo of Nandy asleep by a swimming pool. For a moment, Eugenie could feel her heart stir.

"She's so little," Eugenie said.

"And the world's so big," said Sarah. "Make sure the contact information at the bottom isn't covered."

Sarah's voice sounded a little off, and Eugenie took it to mean she, too, was moved by the disappearance of the little dog.

"Come back to the studio when you're ready for more," Sarah said.

Eugenie took the stack and started for the road. She hadn't gotten far when a car slowed, and the driver honked, shouting, "Oh baby!" as he went by.

On this heavily traveled road, she felt as exposed in yoga clothes as she had at home earlier.

She tacked a few signs to posts and then realized because she was relatively tall, she might have been posting them too high. After all, children could read and they could find Nandy as well as any adult, maybe better. She doubled back over her route and tacked a second sign, this time much lower.

Another car slowed, and she considered, for a second, giving the finger, but then noticed it was Jared's car, and she stopped herself. Through the window, he could be seen pointing in the direction of the studio. Done with the posters Sarah had given her, Eugenie headed toward the parking lot.

She watched as he slowly pulled into an open space. There might be a lot of risks Jared was willing to take, but with his car, he was careful.

"You got it fixed," Eugenie said when she caught up with him.

"Car's a piece of shit, but it's one really beautiful piece of shit," he said. "Didn't expect to see you hitchhiking."

"Posting flyers at Martha's request. Nandy's missing," Eugenie said.

"Who the hell is Nandy?" said Jared.

"The studio dog," said Eugenie. "Martha's dog. The terrier."

"Terrier, poodle, antelope, can't tell one from the other." He looked at her for a moment, and she thought he was going to say something else. When he didn't, Eugenie said, "Well, stuff to do."

"Me, too," he said and turned to walk toward the studio.

 **37**

**EUGENIE WAITED UNTIL** Jared was well inside the door, then realizing he might be hung up at the front desk for a few moments, she decided to bide her time by the side of the building. One non-conversation was about all she could take today.

She hadn't gone far when she came upon a yellow tape. It was strung haphazardly along the length of the side of the studio, looping under some plants and using others to lift it off the ground. Curious, she ducked under a section and proceeded around to the back. There, the yellow tape continued, straighter now as it was secured to an occasional makeshift wooden post.

Eugenie remembered it was a day much like this one when the fire alarm rang out. She looked at the rear doors of the handful of stores that made up the strip mall. Business names were stenciled above each door, valuable for identification but little else. In the middle of each door hung a sign that looked a lot like the alert taped to the studio's front door. She moved closer to read.

A few things stood out. Approved and identifiable personnel were supposed to be watching for signs of smoke and fire. The rear exits were not to be used under any circumstances. Construction was expected.

Eugenie looked around. There had been no attempt at construction that she could see, and Eugenie wondered why. Then she remembered that for work to proceed, each business had to be assessed. Maybe that was the holdup. Then she recalled what Barbara had said about Martha's reaction to being asked for money. Maybe it was Martha herself who was the holdup.

On impulse, Eugenie tried the back door to the studio. It was locked. This was the same door Martha complained was propped open during the ethics class. Maybe the door had been propped open the day Nandy disappeared? Nandy, knowing no better, had taken advantage of what looked like...opportunity? Fun? And then what?

Had one of the personnel mentioned in the sign seen Nandy and taken her? But at that point, wouldn't it have been logical to ask around the strip mall to see if someone had lost a dog? She realized she hadn't posted any "missing" signs here in the back and that probably would be a good idea.

She turned to go back around the side of the building, and something caught her eye - a streak mark directly above the line where rain propelled dirt up the side of the wall. It looked brown. On closer inspection, it looked reddish brown, a little like... Oh no, could it be? She measured the height of the streak against her leg. It was higher than Nandy would have stood. She stared at it for a moment, then decided the streak was just dirt.

Relieved, she headed back to the studio.

# 38

**"THANK VISHNU OR** whoever you're here," said Barbara the minute Eugenie stepped inside.

"More leaflets if you've got them," said Eugenie, careful to stay on the door mat since she had not removed her dirty flip flops.

"No, it's...," said Barbara and gulped.

Eugenie looked at the flushed face and was confused. The lobby was empty, calm even. The doors to the classrooms were closed. Everything was quiet. Even the merchandise for sale on a nearby rack was evenly spaced.

Shattering the mood was Martha who, coming out of her office, misjudged a corner and got tangled in a pair of tights that fell off the hanger and hit the floor.

It was not like Martha to disrespect the merchandise. It must be the dog, thought Eugenie. Martha was upset about the dog.

"Martha, I've been thinking," said Eugenie, "Was Nandy valuable?"

In a very slow voice, as if she were talking to a four-year-old, Martha replied, "Of course, Nandy was valuable. Nandy was my dog, my baby. What a stupid..."

"Yes, to you, valuable," said Eugenie. "But would Nandy have been valuable to someone who didn't know Nandy?"

"If you're thinking you're helping, you couldn't be more wrong. If you really want to help, you'll cover my class. You're the only one dressed for it," said Martha. "There's a client who's not feeling well."

Damn it, thought Eugenie, the only one. If only she hadn't read Martha's text the way she had.

"A class of yours?" said Eugenie, hoping to buy time.

"Of course, a class of mine," said Martha, glancing at the clock on the wall. "A class that should have started seven minutes ago."

"Uh, I guess," said Eugenie.

Looking to Barbara for support, but receiving only a dull, sleep-deprived stare, Eugenie took her flip flops off and eyed the shoe cubby positioned under the tights. The rule was that teachers were to put their shoes in the lowest cubbies, that way the more convenient cubbies were left free for the clients. As none of the upper spaces was available, this was an easy rule to follow today. Eugenie straightened and was halfway to the nearest classroom when Martha cleared her throat and nodded toward the floor.

There lay the crumpled tights. Eugenie was about to say something, thought better of it, then picked them up and hung them in exactly the right place. She moved to the closest classroom door.

"Not that one," Martha said. "The door's closed, which, as you well know, means the class has started."

Eugenie looked around and said, "But all the doors are closed."

Martha moved down the hallway and opened a door. "This one, of course."

Eugenie wasn't sure why she was expected to know Martha's schedule or classroom, but she recognized Martha was in a bind, what with a sick client and a lost dog. And after all, Eugenie did have on the right clothes to teach.

Pulling down her top to cover her hips, Eugenie walked to the door. As Martha left little space between her and the door frame, Eugenie had to suck in her breath in order to pass by.

Pausing, Eugenie asked, "I forgot. The class, what type is it? Beyond your basic yoga, I mean."

"Alignment," said Martha, shutting the door tight.

# 39

**A CROWDED CLASS** already on their feet greeted Eugenie. Since the usual practice was to sit quietly and cross-legged on mats waiting for the teacher to begin, the sight was startling to Eugenie. But quickly, she saw that these students, in their impatience, were way past convention. They spoke in loud voices, and only when she gave her name and mentioned she was covering for Martha did they go silent.

A little too silent for Eugenie's taste. She took in a deep breath and tried to think of what to say.

Alignment was discussed in yoga classes, but "Alignment Yoga" was a whole different animal. It used lots of blocks, that much Eugenie remembered.

"Does everyone have the props they need?" Although no one said, "Yes, we do, and we've had them for the last ten minutes," it was clear from stares and the way this was treated as a rhetorical question that they did.

Eugenie rushed to connect her playlist to Bluetooth, though in her hurry, she dropped her phone twice. Finally, the small screen high on the wall lit up, and lo and behold, there was connection.

In the next instant, the pan flute music she loved came out too loud and with way more confidence than she felt. Nonetheless, Eugenie was determined to rise to the challenge. That is, until she saw who was in the room.

There was more than one model. One Eugenie recognized from a car commercial, another from an air conditioning company ad. The rest were just thin, waiting to be discovered. Alignment Yoga drew these types. The sort who wanted to get everything just right. The type that wanted to make sure they ate 1000 calories per day and not 1001. The type that would not settle for anything less than perfect.

Eugenie suspected she was in big trouble. She decided the only way to cope was to change things up.

"We're going to start with relaxation, backs on mats," Eugenie said.

One of the models started to open her mouth, changed her mind, then sank to her mat. The others, though reluctant, followed suit. Somebody's stomach growled, but in a class like this, what could you expect?

On her phone, Eugenie turned up the volume of the music. If it killed her, she was going to put them in a better mood.

She cued them to tense individual muscles and then relax those same muscles, and she strolled around the room just to make sure they did. Nothing like a teacher standing over a student to inject accountability.

As the class's breathing slowed, Eugenie tried to remember how to teach Alignment Yoga. A picture of Iyengar came to mind. He was the guru who brought Alignment Yoga to the West. And what a fun guy he must have been, thought Eugenie. Every angle the prescribed degree, no more, no less, and hey, to keep you honest, there's the wall. And if off the mark, soon enough, there'll be an adjustment from the teacher.

That was it. She could pick out a few poses, and when everyone was in position, come around and give adjustments. She warmed them up on the mat with a few cat-cow and shoulder stretches and then invited everyone to find a spot on the wall.

"Let's start with triangle! Get yourself into position, both feet touching the baseboard, then go into your spine rotation." The class responded, and to Eugenie's relief, even with all the very long legs, there was enough space.

In the corner, a student wobbled, and Eugenie went to her side. "Okay if I adjust your hip?" asked Eugenie. The woman nodded, and Eugenie bent her knee to provide support to the woman's leg. The last thing Eugenie wanted to do in front of this group was to have a student topple over. She gave the small adjustment and asked the student how that felt. "Good," the woman replied. "Steadier."

The AC company model was next in line, and she self-adjusted just before Eugenie reached her. Louder than was necessary, the model said, "I'm fine, thanks. I don't need any help."

To Eugenie, that was doubtful, but she wasn't going to fight someone who was clearly used to getting her own way.

The class continued with Eugenie providing hip, shoulder, knee, and feet adjustments. It was coming back to her what this alignment stuff was about. That is, until the end of class when the AC company model asked if they could do King Arthur's pose.

King Arthur's pose? Eugenie had never heard of such a thing. And if such a thing existed, what in the world would the Sanskrit be?

"Sure, whatever you want," said Eugenie, still as a statue. The class, realizing Eugenie wasn't going to be of any help as far as cueing, turned their attention to the AC model.

If there was any doubt why this woman had become a model, it was clear now. She relished attention. After a pause to make sure all eyes were on her, she began, "First, kneel with your back to the wall. Then bring one foot out so that leg is in a lunge. Bend the other leg and with one hand, bring it up so the top of the foot rests on the wall. Then scoot that knee back so it's against the wallboard. A great stretch for the quads!"

"Isn't it though," said Eugenie, thinking that if she practiced a hundred years, she would never get herself into that position.

After the pose, there wasn't much else to say or do, and because the wall clock declared time, Eugenie dismissed the class. Chirping exclamations of praise, the students surrounded the model as she left the room.

The props, upended and scattered, like a Lego session gone wrong, were left for Eugenie to put away.

**40**

**GRABBING A BOLSTER,** a Styrofoam block, a sandbag, and a few woven polyester straps, Eugenie headed for the storage closet. There, nothing looked familiar. Whoever had taken the props down in the hasty effort to find Nandy had put them back in an order at once, determined and yet completely inscrutable.

Not wanting to empty the whole closet and start over, Eugenie fell in line with the odd pattern. The bolsters, when gathered from the classroom floor, would have to be stacked to an altitude accessible only by the tallest students. The blocks, when assembled, could only be reached by kneeling on the hard floor.

But the real problem were the rolled-up mats used for the occasional rental. The stack came tumbling down a second after Eugenie realized it was held in place by a book containing meditations for the occasional "off" day.

Appropriate, thought Eugenie, opening then quickly closing the book because there was so much work to do.

On tiptoe, she reached to find an errant strap to add to the other straps, and with it came the bag containing the eye pillows that never, in her experience, had been stored there but, by custom, was tucked in next to the speaker system.

No one had thought to tighten the drawstring around the bag and the eye pillows scattered across the closet floor. Eugenie sighed and considered turning on some high-decibel music so she could allow herself the luxury of screaming without anyone hearing her, but when she heard the door open, she decided against it. She waited for someone to speak, but the only sound was the plop of a Styrofoam block.

Nice, thought Eugenie, they couldn't even walk the five steps to reach the closet and put it away properly.

Irritated, she could no longer resist the book, and she opened and read: "See yourself as surrounded by loved ones or, if that's not possible, a pet, or even a location that brings back good memories."

Immediately, Nandy's face came to mind. The dog's shining eyes, so bright and full of hope, pierced something within Eugenie, and she began to cry. It was then she was glad she'd been left alone to clean up. How could she explain crying for a dog that wasn't even hers? She thought of Nandy out there in the unknown. With a stranger or all alone, she'd be scared, probably bewildered. What had happened to her ordered life?

Nandy liked life just so. If her bowls weren't in the usual place, she would whimper. Eugenie had seen it and had also seen Martha rush to make things right.

Never Ralph, though. He would growl back at the dog and say, "Get used to it," or "Use your nose, for heaven's sake."

Now it was Eugenie's turn to right things. She wiped her eyes with the hem of her top and proceeded to take every single thing off the shelves. On the very back of the top shelf was a stepladder, rusty but probably still usable, and it saved her from perching on shelves that couldn't take her weight. From under the stepladder, she found a towel unused since the last clean-up.

Which was when she realized the top-to-bottom clean of the studio was still days away and she was doing the work of that cleaning company. But what choice did she have at this point? Everything had been taken off the shelves.

Sighing, she yanked at the stepladder's legs. In the attempt to flatten the bar between the legs, she pinched the skin on her fingers. There was no blood, which was good, considering, and she climbed to the top rung, steadying herself by holding on to a shelf. This was actual exercise, she thought to herself, probably what people did to keep themselves fit before there were yoga classes.

To be sure, there was dust on the shelf, but the amount was deceptive. What looked to be only a thin layer was due to the fact it was the same shade as the nondescript paint. One glance at the towel after the initial wipe-down revealed that fact. She coughed as residue not caught by the towel filled the air. She cleared the floor, so the dust had somewhere to land and figured as least then, it could easily be cleaned up. After a few minutes, the floor, her toes, and the green top she wore were all the same color.

Still, she would not be deterred. In her mind's eye, the former configuration of the closet came back, and except for the top shelf, she placed everything back where it was supposed to be.

But then, a problem. How to place a ladder back in its rightful place when it was the ladder she was using? There was no choice but to use a shelf to stand on. With one hand clutching an upper shelf and the other the ladder, she slowly climbed. Her thighs didn't ache or even tremble. Just one more teeny stretch and the ladder would be in place.

It was then she heard a cracking sound.

Not wanting the ladder to come down on her head, she had the presence to let it go. There was no time to adjust her legs, with one getting caught on pillows on the second-to-bottom shelf, leaving the other leg to take the full weight of her descent. The floor, still dusty, was slick, and she fell in a cloudy and extremely loud heap.

There she lay, checking in with each limb to see if it could be moved or screamed pain. Only her head throbbed, and that might be relieved by the ancient stash of pills she kept in the car in the event of cramps. The studio was silent, and for that, she thanked her lucky stars. There was no one to witness her clumsiness.

Still, it was odd. Usually, someone was around, if only Martha, the micro-manager. Nandy's disappearance had changed so much, maybe changed everything.

She reached for the eye pillow bag she had placed exactly where it was supposed to go, right next to the speaker system. It gave her comfort knowing that anyone would know where to find the bag. She emptied the contents on the floor between her splayed legs and took a whiff of the lavender scent of the eye pillows. Lavender could always be depended on to restore one's mood.

Feeling better, she scrambled to her feet and placed the eye pillows back in the bag. All except one. Something was tangled in its ear loops. With some difficulty, she separated the two items and held them in her palms.

Next to the eye pillow was a collar. A dog collar.

And in the center of the collar was a name.

Nandy.

# 41

**AT HOME THAT** night, Eugenie reached for the phone on her bedroom side table. The screen was blank, as blank as her mind felt. She shook it, then pressed a side button or two, and still nothing. Chargeless as her phone was, her body was even more so. And her head still ached. Maybe she had a concussion. No, she was being dramatic, or hysterical, as her mother might have said. An only child wanting to be the center of attention.

Eugenie struggled to the bathroom cabinet, grabbed some aspirin, tried cupping her hand to grab some water from the faucet, and though this had never worked, not once, she flooded her mouth so the pills would go down. As there was precious little water still left in her hand, the pills stayed where they were. She gagged, and the pills went flying, one hitting the mirror with a high-pitched ping, the other sliding down to be caught in the crevice between her breasts under her nightie.

She did have nice breasts. Comments had been made to that effect. And even by one woman on a day Eugenie had treated herself to a spa. Not Jared. Of course, not Jared, who was so obsessed with lust and pain and proving himself that it was unclear to Eugenie if he knew where he was or who he was with.

Which didn't say much for her and her judgment.

She could call Jared, check in, see how he was. She had his number, after all. It might be seen as a considerate gesture, or it might be seen as a booty call, which, despite her headache, was exactly what it was.

Perhaps the fall had dislodged something in her head, something impulsive. She made her way toward the kitchen.

Tripping over a scatter rug, she stopped in her tracks. Things were not the way she left them.

She stood in the center of the kitchen and did a 360. It made her dizzy, and she stopped, her eyes landing on a note tacked to a cabinet.

"Back" was all it said. She squinted and recognized Arabelle's neat script. Once again, her roommate had shown herself to be a woman of few words.

Since oatmeal was the closest thing within reach, Eugenie fixed and downed it so fast it had little time to cool. Throat smarting, she went back to bed, forgetting to swallow the aspirin using an actual glass of water, the reason for coming to the kitchen in the first place.

When she got up again, the headache was gone, and with it, Arabelle.

## 42

**"HEY THERE! YOO-HOO!"**

A man strode in Eugenie's direction. Since she had never seen him in her life, she assumed he was addressing someone else in the crowded parking lot.

"I'm talking to you!" he said, and as if to get her attention, he held out one of two dogs in his arms and waved. The dog's long ears flapped back and forth, covering its eyes.

Eugenie could not help but laugh.

"You're yoga, right?" the man said, out of breath with the weight of the dogs and in his haste to reach her side.

Eugenie looked down at her tights and said, "How d'ya guess?"

The remark seemed to throw him, and instead of answering, he just continued to breathe hard.

"You okay?" Eugenie asked, even though the man was not old or overweight.

"Look, it's the back," he finally answered, using one of the dog's paws to brush his long hair out of his eyes.

"The back? You mean *your* back?" Eugenie said. "Oh, there are plenty of classes for that."

"My back? No, no. My back's fine," he said. "Could you hold one of these?"

Without waiting for her to answer, he handed over a dog. It squirmed and twisted, and before she knew it, the creature had pulled down her top, exposing a hanging-on-for-dear-life sports bra.

Something in the man's eyes softened, and after several seconds, he said, "Sorry, I forgot what I was saying."

"Look, I have class," said Eugenie. "Something about the back. What back?"

"The back! Yes! The back of the complex. The back of all our businesses. The back of the strip mall. The back which is tie-a-yellow-ribboned off. The back!"

"Ah, well, it may be the back of your business, but it's not mine. I'm no owner. Only one of the teachers," said Eugenie.

"I see," he said and slumped for a moment, then recovered. "But you know him or her, the owner, that is."

"Well, of course, yes. I work for her," said Eugenie.

"Then you have influence. Clout, you might say," said the man.

"Clout is the one thing I would definitely not say," said Eugenie.

"If you could just talk to her. We need to get this thing off the ground," said the man.

"What thing off the...?" said Eugenie.

"She needs to pay!" said the man. "The rest of us have. Paid the assessment, that is. For the work to be done. I need my back door back. Or the animals do. To do their business."

"Business? Who are you anyway?" said Eugenie.

"The vet. That's me," he said, pointing to a sign over a storefront that read, "Xavier Kip, Veterinarian to Cats and Dogs." Then, in a more serious tone, he said, "And this one needs to pee."

"Oh, you mean the dog," said Eugenie, looking around the parking lot. "Ah, okay. Where would you suggest?"

"Exactly my point," said Xavier. "The back needs to be fixed so we can use the rear door to get to the grass."

Eugenie began to hand the dog back, but it wiggled, letting out a blast of urine, which quickly soaked her front.

Xavier reacted as if this happened every day and took the dog back with a little shake, shake, shake.

"Talk to her!" said Xavier. "Tell her if I can pay off my damn school loans on top of paying for the assessment, then by golly, she can ante up."

Eugenie watched as he stomped away and wondered. Who said by golly, anyway?

# 43

**EUGENIE LEANED AGAINST** a studio wall in the hope she could avoid touching the urine stain and take off her flip flops at the same time without falling on her ass.

"Martha?" she yelled out. She wanted to tell her about finding Nandy's collar.

There was no answer.

"Anybody?" she tried.

Eugenie straightened to find an empty lobby. "Where the hell is everybody?"

She looked around and finding an empty bathroom, her annoyance turned to relief. At least there was no one to witness the state she was in. She took off her top and bra, and with a paper towel doused with water and hand soap, she cleaned her front. In between wipes, she let out a little "Yuck."

Deed done, she realized she still had a class coming up. And therefore, needed something to wear.

The merchandise on the rack! She would grab something and pay for it later, out of her paycheck.

She snatched some fresh paper towels and pressing them to her chest, she headed into the lobby toward the rack.

It was her luck that Jared was coming in the front door at the same time.

"Oh honey," he said, eyes wide. "You read my mind."

"Shut up," said Eugenie. "I have class."

"Nude yoga?" said Jared. "Heard about that. Didn't realize it was offered here."

Eugenie rolled her eyes. In her surprise at seeing Jared, the paper towels had toppled to the floor. She quickly covered her breasts with an arm, and with the other, she grabbed the largest top she could find from the rack and raced back into the bathroom.

The top was a color she would have avoided under normal circumstances, but an even worse drawback was the size. Though the tag read "L," in yoga world, that might mean large but could also mean anything from petite to medium. With several tugs, she finally got it over her head and shoulders. As for her breasts, she was relieved to find the top so tight, no sports bra was needed, but dismayed to see it left a strip of belly over her tights plainly visible.

Still in the lobby when she returned, Jared brightened.

"Don't you have somewhere to be?" Eugenie asked. "I know I do."

"Wouldn't miss this show for anything," said Jared, who went quiet as soon as he noticed Martha coming through the front door.

He nodded to Martha, who gave Eugenie an odd look and simultaneously pointed at her wristband and mouthed to Jared, "Time!"

# 44

**THE ONLY STUDENTS** in class were either near-sighted or too polite to mention Eugenie's attire. Since being called on to cover for Sarah at the last moment, Eugenie had taken time to memorize a sequence of poses. Now, she was relieved to rely on it: warm up gently, then do eight asanas that needed little to no explanation to anyone who'd ever taken a yoga class, and finally, a long, very long in the case of this class, savasana.

No one complained, and she soon found herself back in the parking lot trying to find where she'd parked her car.

White or silver cars were so common in this hot part of the world, her car often had, in a parking lot of any size, a dozen look-alikes. Then she remembered she had parked in front of the vet's. There it was!

And there also was Jared.

Relaxed from the class, she would try and be nice.

"How was your session with Martha?" asked Eugenie.

"Great. I'm thinking of firing my physical therapist. Except for one thing," he said, pointing to the studio. "She's morose."

"Wow," said Eugenie. "That's a two-dollar word if I ever heard one."

"Hey, I read the newspaper," said Jared. "Sometimes. The sports page anyway. Well, football. Well, college football."

"So, who's morose?" said Eugenie.

"Martha, of course," said Jared.

"Because of the dog?" said Eugenie.

"That...and other things," said Jared. "She wants you to handle things for a while."

A car on a side street braked hard, drowning out his words.

"Did you hear what I said?" said Jared. "She wants you to..."

A roar from a plane on the flight path to the airport made Eugenie cover her ears.

"I said," said Jared, "SHE WANTS YOU TO RUN THE STUDIO!"

The parking lot was now so quiet his words made her jump.

"I thought you said she wants me to run the studio," said Eugenie, laughing.

"Handle shit for a while, yes," said Jared.

Eugenie continued to laugh until something in Jared's expression made her stop.

"You're not joking," said Eugenie.

"No, I'm not," said Jared.

"Well, she's said nothing about it," said Eugenie.

"She ran it by me first," said Jared.

"By you?" said Eugenie. "Why by you?"

"Trusts my judgment," said Jared, to which Eugenie could give no reply.

"Well," said Jared, "Got to run. The rehabilitated life calls!"

Eugenie leaned against the hood of her car, which, in the heat, stung the exposed flesh on her back.

"Ouch," she said to no one in particular.

**45**

**IN HER CAR,** Eugenie turned on the air conditioner and turned off her cell phone. If there were messages, she didn't want to see them. Her head throbbed and her heart raced. She was soon at the burger place across the street.

"Will you be eating in your car, or...?" the voice said from the box under the menu.

"Car. In the car. In my car," said Eugenie.

"A Toyota," said the voice.

"How do you know?" said Eugenie.

"We've spoken, though you haven't been here for a while," said the voice.

It never occurred to Eugenie she would be recognized at this place. One of the things she liked about drive-thru fast food was anonymity.

"Then the usual," said Eugenie.

"A while means chances are good, I've forgotten your usual," said the voice.

Eugenie gave her order, then realizing it sounded like a lot for one person, added she was getting food for friends.

"You don't have to explain. We're a judgment-free zone," said the voice.

Embarrassed, Eugenie considered pulling out of line, but there was no place to go. Reluctantly, she inched up to the delivery window.

"You're not the person I was just speaking to," Eugenie said to the employee.

"No," said the young woman, "I just give out the food. At least today, I give out the food. Tomorrow, who knows? I might be taking the orders. You've never heard of cross-training? Well, that's the way we do things here."

"Cross-training, sure I've heard of it," said Eugenie, who hadn't. "Who was the person I was just speaking to, the one who took my order?"

"Probably Quincy. The manager," she said with more than just a little pride.

"He sounds nice," said Eugenie.

"He is nice," said the young woman. "But you have to be that way if you're the manager."

"A hard job," said Eugenie.

"The hardest," said the young woman. "You wouldn't believe the flack he has to take. Not from me, but from..."

The driver in the car behind Eugenie, seeing that she had paid and received her food, flashed headlights.

Eugenie gave a wave to the young woman, released the brake, and pressed down on the accelerator.

Almost hitting Martha, who at that moment was crossing the lot, clothed not in spandex but in a dress. In her hand, she gripped a suitcase, sale tag still dangling from the handle.

## 46

FOR AS LONG as she dared, Eugenie kept her phone turned off. Then, in the early morning hours, while staring at herself in the bathroom mirror, she pressed the power button.

And there it was. A text from Martha.

"Do what's necessary," it said.

Not a thank you. Not even a please. And starting when, wondered Eugenie. And for how long? It had never occurred to Eugenie that Martha liked her enough to trust her with running the studio which bore her name.

Eugenie tried several times to go back to sleep, but when that was not possible, she got up and showered. She drove to the studio parking lot, and remembering the alligator, she circled several times, hoping to create enough noise to startle any lurking creature back into the wild.

At the studio, she entered the code in the security pad, opened the door, and tripped on something metallic. It skittered across the floor, leaving a trail of water.

Barbara looked up from the desk and said, "Nandy's water and food bowl."

Eugenie, eyes wide, said, "Nandy's come back? But that's wonderful."

Barbara, looking like it took more energy than she had, shook her head. Then Ralph, looking equally lethargic, came out of the office.

"So, what's going on?" said Eugenie. "Why the food and water?"

"In the hope that Nandy will return," said Ralph. "Wishful thinking on Martha's part. One way of putting it."

Eugenie hesitated, not quite knowing what to say. Finally, raising the phone in her hand, she said, "I got a text."

"We know," said Barbara, stifling a yawn. "Why we're here. Organizing things so you don't make too much of a mess. Oh yeah, there's this," said Barbara, handing Eugenie an envelope.

"Look guys," said Eugenie. "I didn't ask to run things. Either of you is way more qualified."

"Right," said Barbara. "Me being here a total of what, almost a week."

"Or me, being the fucking husband," said Ralph.

"I mean, I have no idea. I've never been a manager," said Eugenie.

"Bet I know what will convince you," said Barbara. "The envelope. Open it."

Eugenie threaded a finger under the flap and received a paper cut for her effort. "Ow," she said, sucking on the skin.

"Never mind," said Ralph. "Open it."

Eugenie finally got the envelope open and peeked inside just long enough to see a stack of bills.

"Money?" said Eugenie. "From Martha?"

Ralph and Barbara nodded, as if they were witnessing some solemn event.

"Okay, already clueless. What's the deal with paying cash?" said Eugenie.

"Don't spend it all in one place," said Barbara. "You can never tell with Martha. She may ask for it back. That is, if Nandy isn't found."

# 47

**A FEW MINUTES** later came the sound of soft knocks from the studio front door.

Eugenie looked at the wall clock and said to Barbara, "Who could that be? We don't open for another hour."

Barbara looked blank, and if possible, even worse than she had when Eugenie entered the studio.

Ralph just shook his head and went back into the office and shut the door.

The sound of knocking continued.

Eugenie started for the door, then saw Barbara get up from her chair and slump headfirst onto the front desk.

"Barbara!" said Eugenie, heading back in her direction.

The sound of knocking got louder, and then a young voice said, "I've got your dog. Hey! I've found your dog."

Eugenie yelled out, "Wait a minute!" Then, lowering Barbara to the floor, she said, "Just wait!" Racing around, Eugenie found a blanket someone had left on the counter and tucked it under Barbara's head. Barbara's eyes were shut, but a check of her pulse proved she was alive.

"Your dog! I've found it," said the voice.

"Ralph, we could use some help out here," said Eugenie. "Ralph!" When he didn't respond, she checked Barbara again and was relieved to find her eyes now open.

"Oh Barbara," said Eugenie, "Thank goodness!"

"Your dog is here!" said the voice as Eugenie dashed to the studio door. Opening it, she found a boy with a squirming dog in his arms. From a nearby car, a woman waved. This, Eugenie assumed, was the mother.

"Lady," said the boy. "I saw the sign and I can read! Here's your dog."

The look in his eyes as he passed the creature to Eugenie was full of delight and accomplishment. From behind him, the woman yelled, "Come on, kiddo! No asking for a reward. We've got to get going."

"A reward," said Eugenie, "Well now, yes, let me just think." But before she knew it, the boy was back in the vehicle which quickly pulled away from the curb.

Eugenie watched them go, shaking her head at their kindness.

Unfortunately, before the car had exited the parking lot and before she'd even closed the studio door, she knew the one thing she wished she didn't.

The dog in her arms was not Nandy.

# 48

A MINUTE AFTER his paws touched the floor, the dog toppled Nandy's water bowl and dug its nose deep into the food bowl.

Ralph opened the office door and said, "Could you keep it down? I'm trying to get some work done."

Hearing his voice, the dog ran to his side.

"Oh good," said Ralph, "Nandy's back. That's one less thing to worry about."

"Take a second look," said Eugenie, squeezing behind the front desk so she could get to Barbara.

"Yeah, I see what you mean," said Ralph, reaching down to stop the dog from going into the office. "Maybe she won't notice."

"Martha?" said Eugenie. "Her own dog, and she won't notice if it's hers or not?"

Ralph skirted the dog and peeked over the desk. "What are you doing down there, Eugenie?"

"She's attending to me," said Barbara.

"And Barbara," said Ralph. "You're on the ground. What are you doing on the ground?"

"Shit," said Barbara. "Can we just kill him?"

Eugenie took in a deep breath and said, "Barbara fainted. I helped her to the floor. I yelled for you. A little boy came to the door and dropped off a dog, thinking it was Martha's lost dog from the flyers. And you," Eugenie took in another deep breath. "You just stayed put while all this was going on."

"Hey, not like I'm doing nothing. Trying to find a password, several as a matter of fact," said Ralph.

"Ralph," said Eugenie. "Help me get Barbara up. I'm going to take her home."

"She can't go home," said Ralph. "There's too much to do. Plus the fact, she knows, well, too much."

Barbara raised her head slightly and said, "Remind me to mention that fact if Martha decides to fire me."

"Shush," said Eugenie. "Just relax. Ralph, come over to the other side, and let's get Barbara to her feet."

Ralph did as he was told, but looked as if Eugenie had asked him to touch a stool sample.

"On my count," said Eugenie. "One, two, three!"

Eugenie lifted, taking the bulk of Barbara's weight. Her back groaned with the effort.

"Sorry," said Ralph. "I thought there would be a 'four' after the 'three.' Isn't there always a four after the three?"

"I repeat," said Barbara, "Can't we just..."

"Don't concern yourself," said Eugenie to Barbara. "We need to get you home and better."

"But the passwords, I only know a few!" said Ralph.

Barbara, held up by Eugenie, turned slightly in his direction. "No worries. They all start with A. S. S. H.O.L..."

**49**

**EUGENIE FOUND BARBARA'S** house without too much trouble. It wasn't far from hers, so when Barbara, sprawled on the back seat, gave directions, she didn't have to say them twice.

"Sure you don't want me to take you to urgent care?" said Eugenie, pulling into Barbara's driveway. "There's one not far away."

"No," said Barbara, looking out the window. "My partner will take me to the doctor. Already texted made an appointment."

Eugenie got out of the car to offer her hand and was surprised at the force with which Barbara took it.

"About Ralph," said Eugenie. "Don't feel you have to apologize or anything."

"I wasn't," said Barbara, opening the front door to the house. "Going to apologize or anything."

Eugenie couldn't help but laugh, then said, "You don't lock it?"

"If we don't remember, we don't," said Barbara, flopping down on a couch in an open area that appeared to serve as living room, dining room, and kitchen. "My partner thinks this is such a swell neighborhood, private property can't help but be respected."

"Really?" said Eugenie, trying hard not to show her surprise.

"Yeah, I know," said Barbara. "Guess it's what you're used to."

"Everything's relative," said Eugenie.

"Spoken like the yoga teacher she is," said Barbara, lying back on mismatched pillows and a stack of folded underwear.

"You don't look well," said Eugenie.

"Your CPR training up to date?" said Barbara.

Eugenie had to think for a moment. "The last time I took the re-cert class was at the studio. Martha's idea to hold one there. She thought it would be more convenient for the teachers."

"Woman has her moments," said Barbara.

"Look," said Eugenie. "Can I get you anything?"

"Water," said Barbara, pointing. "There's some filtered in the pitcher on the counter."

Eugenie opened a few cupboards and found a glass. She lifted the pitcher to pour and a piece of paper under it fell to the floor. Picking it up, she turned it over. It was a poor copy of a photo. It took a moment, but it dawned on her this was the same picture the security guard had shown her and Ralph when they were sitting in his car.

Eugenie handed the glass to Barbara who took a deep draw, choking a few times as the water made its way down.

"You wouldn't by any chance have an aspirin?" said Barbara. "My head's killing me."

"I carry some somewhere," said Eugenie, "But until you see the doctor, you probably shouldn't take anything."

"Thanks a lot, Mom," said Barbara, looking down at her phone. "You can go. My partner's almost here."

"Oh," said Eugenie. "If you're sure."

"I'm sure," said Barbara. "Go."

"Keep in touch," said Eugenie. "There's paper on the counter. I'm going to leave my cell number just in case."

A pencil hung by a string from the refrigerator handle and Eugenie used it to scribble down her info on the back of the photo.

In a minute, she was pulling out of the driveway and onto the street. At the intersection, she braked sharply, avoiding by inches, a car running the stop sign.

The driver looked a lot like Fritzi.

# 50

**"NO NEED TO** go on. Your order's etched in my brain by now," said the voice from the box.

"Quincy, the manager?" said Eugenie. "I'm having a bad day."

"Nothing a cheeseburger couldn't help?" said Quincy.

"Maybe, still...," said Eugenie.

"I'm compiling things fast as I can. Fries are almost up," said Quincy.

"Thanks," said Eugenie. "But it's business help I really need. You can't believe what's happened and I've just started."

"Hold on, hold on," said Quincy. "There's several burgers need flipping."

"Of course," said Eugenie. "I was just hoping that you, as a manager, could give me some tips. You see, an employee who..."

"Skip the details," said Quincy. "See that line behind you?"

"Yes," said Eugenie. "But could you see your way to give one tip that might help a new manager?"

"I'm thinking," said Quincy, and a car behind Eugenie honked.

A cacophony of noise issued from the speaker. Eugenie could make out voices, some insistent.

"Is everything okay?" Eugenie asked.

"Inconceivable!" said Quincy. "A burger joint and not a stitch of ketchup to be found."

"Want me to go to a store and get you some?" said Eugenie.

"You're kindness itself," said Quincy. "But we need the packets. The regulation packets. The packets that come from the warehouse in Atlanta."

A second horn blasted from a car behind Eugenie.

"Take mine and give them to someone else," said Eugenie. "If that's any help."

"'Tis, my lady," said Quincy.

A woman's hand clutching some bags extended out the pickup window and almost hit Eugenie in the cheek.

"Here," she said. "And oh yeah. I don't know why this means anything, but the boss said to tell you, 'Expect the unexpected.'"

**51**

**EUGENIE FINISHED THE** last bite of food in the parking lot. She knew she would reek of fat when she entered the studio, but she didn't care. She needed every calorie to have the talk she intended with Ralph.

Getting out of the car she had parked deliberately in Martha's spot, Eugenie popped the fast-food bags with a satisfying bang and headed toward the studio.

She hadn't taken three steps before a man in a white lab jacket came running toward her. She tucked the bags behind her back, but not before he had thrown his arms around her in a bear hug.

"Hey, no, stop!" she said, freeing herself in one fell swoop.

"Xavier Kip," said the man, letting her loose without taking offense. "You must remember. Xavier Kip. Vet to dogs and cats or vet to cats and dogs, depending on your preference." And he pointed to the sign above his store in exactly the same way he did the last time.

"Oh, yes," Eugenie said. "I remember. There's been a lot going on."

"I'll say," said Xavier. "You're magic."

"If you say so," said Eugenie, who backed up when she noticed a pink nose peeking out of his lab jacket and heading straight for the bags in her hand.

Xavier looked down and laughed. "Better sense of smell than twenty of us. Here, you want to hold?"

Remembering what happened the last time he handed over an animal, Eugenie said, "No."

"Speaks her mind," said Xavier. "I like that. That how you handled the studio owner?"

Eugenie wondered if the stress of the day and the fat she'd just ingested were getting to her. From out of the corner of her eye, she saw Ralph, holding open the door of the studio and frantically waving at her.

"I got to go," said Eugenie.

"Not before I give thanks," said Xavier.

Ralph was shouting now, something incomprehensible.

"Look," said Eugenie, "I've never 'handled' as you say, Martha about anything. I have no idea what you're talking about."

"And modest too," said Xavier. "Well, let me just say thank you." And, looking toward the animal in his pocket, he said, "Philomena says thank you too."

# 52

"**WHAT IS IT,** Ralph?" said Eugenie, racing toward him, missing by inches the decorative pot on the walkway before she sailed through the open studio door.

"The phone," said Ralph. "An important call."

Eugenie reached toward the cell in his hand and said, "Oh God. Not about Barbara."

"Who's Barbara?" said Ralph.

Eugenie pointed to the floor behind the desk and said, "On-the-floor Barbara. Fainted-Barbara."

"Oh her," said Ralph, holding on tight to the phone in his hand. "No."

"Then who?" said Eugenie. "And why are you not giving me the phone if it's so important?"

"Not my cell!" said Ralph. "The landline, of course. On the desk. Line one. Well, the only one that's lit."

Eugenie rounded the desk, pressed the button, and held the receiver to her ear. A dial tone was all she heard.

"There's no one on it," said Eugenie, extending the phone so he could hear.

"You probably disconnected the call," said Ralph. "When's the last time you used a landline?"

"Ages," said Eugenie, "But I didn't. It was disconnected from the other side. Who was it anyway?"

"Martha," said Ralph.

"Martha?" said Eugenie. "She say anything to you?"

"Nothing repeatable," said Ralph.

"Ralph, I need to talk with her," said Eugenie. "I, we, have no idea what we're doing. Some direction's what's needed."

"You're telling me," said Ralph.

"Then what's her number?" said Eugenie.

"No idea," said Ralph.

"You're making no sense," said Eugenie. "How can you not know her number?"

"It's changed. Like a lot of things," said Ralph, his shoulders slumping.

"Look, isn't there some way to get the number from this phone?" Eugenie said, pointing to the one on the desk. "It looks techie enough."

"There is, but it's not like I can help you with all the stuff I have to do," said Ralph.

She wanted to shake him. "What is going on?" said Eugenie. "You don't seem like yourself."

Ralph shook his head as if he were as confounded as she. Then, after a pause, he said, "Oh yeah, and you know that dog, the one that isn't Nandy. It's missing too."

# 53

RALPH SLUNK BACK into the office, leaving Eugenie to scour the studio. She tried calling out, "Doggie!" because as far as she knew, the dog could be called anything. Then, feeling silly, she tried, "Max! Milo! Buddy!" And then, realizing she didn't know the sex of the dog, she tried, "Cleo!" then "Milly!"

The whole thing was ridiculous. The dog had been dropped off, wasn't even theirs, and they'd already lost it. The dog had nothing to do with the studio and yet, here she was, racing around like a maniac. Regardless, she entered each of the three classrooms to rule them out, then both bathrooms, and the closets, and by the time she got to the library, she felt like an utter fool. She stood with her hands on her hips and sighed and that's when Ralph peaked out of the office and yelled, "I forgot. Maybe outside?"

Good heavens, thought Eugenie. The back doors were, according to the fire department, not to be used. She wasn't even sure if the back door could be opened, but quickly, she found out it could. She peeked out.

Several stores down from the studio stood Xavier who seeing her, waved back and then pointing to some earth-moving equipment, gave a thumbs up. She hadn't realized work was beginning. Which must mean, she thought... But the thought had no time to materialize when off to her left came a small creature sprinting toward her. With one impressive leap, the dog jumped into her startled arms and then, in quick succession, the rustle of something long and heavy tore at the brush in the distance.

Eugenie ducked back inside and slammed the door, her heart pumping.

She dropped the dog by the water bowl and said to Ralph, "You let the dog go outside? By itself?"

Ralph looked sheepish and said, "What do you want from me? It had to go."

"You know what's out there," said Eugenie. "We both know."

"Martha said it wasn't one," said Ralph, "So maybe it wasn't, isn't."

"Well, you may not know," said Eugenie, "But I do."

Eugenie looked out the front window and saw some trucks pulling into the parking lot. "Honestly! The stuff that goes on around this place!" she said to Ralph.

Outside, she waved to one of the truck drivers, who seemed more than happy to stop for Eugenie. It was then she realized how she must look. She tugged down at her yoga top and up at her yoga tights.

"What can I do for you, missy?" said the driver, his massive head and shoulder taking up most of the open window of the truck.

Eugenie ignored the missy bit and said, "You part of the crew doing the work behind the stores?"

"I am. We're just getting started," said the driver.

"You know about the...," said Eugenie. "I mean you know there might be an...," she almost added and then was scared to say the word.

"Alligator?" said the driver.

"Yes," said Eugenie. "Oh, my goodness, that means you've seen it!"

"No," said the driver. "Haven't seen it."

"Then why did you say alligator?" said Eugenie.

"Because," said the driver, "Anywhere around here there's water, there could be gators. That's just the way it is."

"Can you?" said Eugenie. "Would you?"

"Get rid of it?" said the driver.

"I don't mean kill it," said Eugenie.

"What do you mean then?" said the driver. "Invite it to tea?"

"No, no, nothing like that," said Eugenie, embarrassed. "I mean, find it another home."

The driver laughed and shook his head. "You're kidding. Look missy, if we find a gator, trust the guys know what to do. We know exactly what to do."

"Oh good," said Eugenie. "Call the fish and wildlife people."

"Yeah, sure," said the driver, still laughing as he pulled away. "Exactly what I was thinking."

# 54

**SARAH HAD SNUCK** into the studio while Eugenie was talking to the driver.

"You won't believe my day!" said Sarah, taking off her sandals, as Eugenie came in the door.

She stole the words right out of Eugenie's mouth.

"You're looking stressed," said Sarah. "Here to take my class? Smart. Best thing for the nervous system."

Eugenie tried not to show her irritation but doubted she was successful. Sarah had not even asked what Eugenie was doing there. She just assumed it was for her class.

"Go ahead," said Ralph from behind the desk. "I'll keep an eye on things."

Unlikely as that was, Eugenie could not come up with an excuse, and headed toward a classroom.

"Not that one," said Sarah. "No way my class could ever fit in that small room."

Of course, thought Eugenie. Sarah was a living, breathing advertisement for yoga. Work your spine and you, too can look like me.

Eugenie entered a larger room and retrieved a mat from the closet and spread it on the floor.

"You forgot yours today?" said Sarah, following her in.

Eugenie had, but she wasn't going to admit that to Sarah. "In the car. I'll just use this one."

Sarah surveyed the mat and asked, "Whose job is it to clean these, anyway? You know, disinfect them? Think of the sweat and fuck, the snot."

Eugenie didn't want to think of those things. She didn't even want to think.

"What class is this, anyway?" said Eugenie.

"Oh, I forget what it's officially called," said Sarah. "You know Martha with her creative names. But it's easy."

The classroom was now so crowded with students the edge of their mats touched.

Sarah strode to the front of the room, eyeing the mats on either side of hers with such distaste that both students hopped up to move them.

"Better," said Sarah. "Let's start."

The first fifteen minutes went okay for Eugenie, but the rest of the class was torture. Eugenie wondered if Sarah was deliberately making it as hard as possible simply because Eugenie was there. By the end of class, Eugenie was soaked.

"See now, don't you feel better?" said Sarah as Eugenie was about to put the mat back in the closet.

"Not there," said Sarah. "It has to be cleaned before it's put back. Maybe Ralph knows what to do."

Eugenie thought, if Ralph knows what to do, it will be the first time.

**55**

**IN HER CAR** on the way home, Eugenie was so tired she almost fell asleep waiting for a light to turn green. The driver behind her let her know to get moving by honking.

Pulling into the driveway, all she could think about was shower, then bed. Or maybe just bed.

It was not to be. Arabelle stood at the kitchen counter chopping up something with an energy Eugenie could only envy and Eugenie, in her bare feet, tried to tiptoe past her.

"What's up?" said Arabelle, unaccountably adding the word, "Pal."

"Nothing," said Eugenie. "Just bed."

"Are you kidding?" said Arabelle. "Sun's not even down."

"I know," said Eugenie, unwilling or unable to explain.

"I've made something that'll make you feel like superwoman," said Arabelle.

"No," said Eugenie.

"Ah, c'mon," said Arabelle. "We got to keep you going."

"No," said Eugenie, more harshly than she meant. Then again, "No."

"Okay, okay, geez," said Arabelle. "It'll keep. I'll put some in the frig for you."

Eugenie was too tired to even say thanks. She made her way to the shower, and with some difficulty, yanked off her sweat-soaked tights and top. The sports bra was her undoing. It clung to her breasts at odd angles, then got caught on the flesh around a shoulder. She briefly considered asking Arabelle to help, but that was a lot to ask of a tenant. She would sacrifice the sports bra by cutting it with scissors if it came to that. But with one last tug, it finally slid up her arms.

She turned the shower on cold and didn't flinch when the water hit her. She wondered if the temperature would revive her, but her exhaustion was so great, it didn't make a dent. She threw on an oversized t-shirt she'd gotten free from some event and hit the mattress.

And it was there that Eugenie's mind, against all odds, went into overdrive.

## 56

**STARING UP AT** a ceiling known as 1950s popcorn, Eugenie's eyes were wide open, as if toothpicks propped the lids.

In the stream of light coming from the slit between the curtains, she could make out a small spider climbing up and down the bumpy ceiling. It must seem like a trip across the Pyrenees, thought Eugenie.

Which is what her life seemed like now. The crossing of a mountain range.

Why had Martha left so suddenly? Why had Martha paid Eugenie with cash? Why in the world had Martha put Eugenie in charge?

What was up with Ralph? She'd never seen him so moody.

How was Barbara doing and why hadn't she heard from her?

Where, oh where, was Nandy?

And for heaven's sake, if Eugenie was to manage the studio, someone had better come up with the passwords and fast.

These questions seemed as difficult to answer as what was the meaning of life and why do we die? Under the sheet, she picked at a bit of skin dangling from her big toe.

She turned on the bedside light and examined her feet. She couldn't remember when she'd gotten her last pedicure and the polish on the nails was chipped.

There would be no time for that tomorrow. She had an early class and then somehow, she had to get a handle on the running of the studio.

She thought of Quincy, the burger place manager. He had a nice voice, but beyond that, she didn't know much. She envisioned him as tall, slender and tall, but maybe that was because Jared was slender and tall.

She thought of how Jared had passed on Martha's message, about her becoming the manager. That still seemed odd. Why did Martha trust Jared of all people to deliver the message?

Had Martha abandoned the studio to look for Nandy and if she had, why didn't she just say so?

On the side chest of drawers, Eugenie's phone pulsed. She considered ignoring it. After all, her parents were dead, and she had no other family. What could be so important that someone would reach out to her at this time of day?

And then she remembered she was now the studio's manager. She read the text.

"Coming in tomorrow," was all it said.

In her exhaustion, she couldn't imagine who the sender might be. When people shared their phone numbers, she usually added their names to the contact list on her phone. But not always.

"Barbara?" texted Eugenie back.

"Y," came the answer.

"Glad to hear from you," texted Eugenie. "I was worried. Are you sure about tomorrow?"

Thumbs up, texted Barbara. Then, "I'm sure. Very sure. Got a bone to pick with Ralph."

Eugenie thought about answering back that Ralph might be there, then again maybe not. He hadn't been in the most predictable of moods. But if Barbara knew that, she might not come in. And more than anything else, Eugenie needed Barbara at the studio.

Eugenie looked at her phone and with an enthusiasm she didn't feel, she pressed a smiley face emoji.

## 57

**EUGENIE ARRIVED AT** the studio parking lot, looked around for alligators, and, seeing none, walked to the front door. As she was partway through entering the security code numbers, the door opened.

"Ralph!" said Eugenie.

"I'll have to give you the new code," said Ralph.

"Oh," said Eugenie. "You mean..."

"Soon the old one won't work," said Ralph.

Taking off her flip flops and placing them in a cubby, Eugenie said, "So you're changing it?"

"Two can play at that game," said Ralph.

"What game?" said Eugenie to Ralph who waved his hand as if to shoo the question away.

"And what two?" said Eugenie to Ralph, who in his determination not to answer almost tripped over the dog that still wasn't Nandy.

"Look Ralph," said Eugenie. "It's possible Barbara might actually be able to help out around here and if that's the case, we need her."

"What we need," said Ralph, "Is to get rid of the dog."

"You mean find a loving and stable home for the dog," said Eugenie.

"Right," said Ralph. "The vet down the way opens soon. I'm going to see if I can drop him or her or whatever off."

"Oh, you mean Xavier Kip?" said Eugenie.

"Got me," said Ralph, giving Eugenie a look. "Only know there's a vet."

"I'll go," said Eugenie.

"Such an eager beaver," said Ralph. "Just don't come back with it. What we don't need around here is one more thing to take care of."

Eugenie looked down to see the water and food bowls were empty. As far as she could see, there wasn't much taking care of being done, at least not by Ralph.

## 58

**AFTER FINDING SOME** food for the dog, Eugenie gathered the little one up in her arms and walked down to Xavier's office. At the entrance, the vet was occupied trying to pick out a key from a crowded ring and without looking up, he said, "If you think this is a clinic, it's not. It's a practice which means appointments are to be made. In advance."

Eugenie laughed uncomfortably and after he found a key to fit in the lock, he glanced over at her.

"Oh, it's you," he said. "Exceptions made for angels of mercy. Come in!"

He held the door open, and Eugenie walked into a spic and span reception area. The air smelled of chemicals.

"Wow," said Eugenie. "Nice place you got here."

"Cleaning crew probably left about an hour ago. Don't know what I'd do without them," said Xavier. "Animals carry all kinds of disease."

"People, too," said Eugenie, thinking she must remember to find out how the mats and the bathrooms were cleaned.

Xavier took the bag from his shoulder and dropped it on the counter. From a hook on the wall, he retrieved a lab coat and slowly put it on over a blue shirt. The minute he did, it was clear white didn't favor him the way blue did.

"What have you got there?" said Xavier, flipping on light switches.

"I'm not sure," said Eugenie. "It was dropped off at the studio. By a little boy."

"Okay," said Xavier. "I'm lost. Why, why, and why?"

"The kid was trying to be helpful," said Eugenie. "The studio did lose a dog. Or rather, the manager Martha Wetherell did. Nandy's the dog's name, and it was kind of the studio's mascot. Anyway, when Martha discovered her dog was missing, she enlisted the teachers to post notices along the streets around here. The boy said he saw one of the signs and, thinking this was the dog that was lost, dropped it off at the studio."

"Okay, still confused," said Xavier. "When you saw it wasn't the right dog, why didn't you tell him?"

"It was busy, and I was distracted. And he looked so pleased with himself. And his mother was outside in a car waiting for him. And...," said Eugenie. "Truth is I really don't know much about dogs. It took me a moment to take in the fact it wasn't Nandy."

"So, you're adopting," said Xavier. "And you want me to check the little guy out."

Eugenie suddenly wished with all her heart she had not volunteered to bring the dog but had let Ralph do it. Ralph wouldn't have cared what Xavier thought.

"No," Eugenie said softly. "I thought you might know what to do."

"This isn't a pet shelter, you know," said Xavier. "This is a professional veterinarian practice."

"I'm sorry," said Eugenie. "You're right. I just thought..."

Xavier stood with his hands on hips, looking nonplussed. He paced the length of the reception area once, twice, then a third time.

"If it were anyone else," he finally said.

"I just thought you might know...," said Eugenie.

"If it were anyone else," Xavier repeated, "I wouldn't hesitate to show you the door. But you got the work started on the back of the strip and I'm grateful."

Eugenie wondered if she should tell him she had no idea why the work on the back started. Then the dog began wiggling like crazy. In her arms, it strained in the direction of Xavier. She hoped it was a sign. Oh dear, Eugenie thought, she was becoming her mother, believing things to be signs.

"So, you'll take it?" said Eugenie.

He said nothing, just extended his arms, one hand brushing along her forearm.

It was then, she couldn't help but notice, her skin experienced a definite tingle.

## 59

**WHEN EUGENIE ARRIVED** back at the studio empty-handed, she thought Ralph would be pleased. But if anything, his mood was worse. Oh no, thought Eugenie, had he and Barbara had words?

She looked around, taking a few minutes to check the props closet, the library, and the bathroom.

"What are you doing?" said Ralph who had crept up behind her.

"Barbara," said Eugenie. "Where is she?"

"Not here," said Ralph.

"Why?" said Eugenie. "She said she'd be here today. Is she not okay?"

"No," said Ralph. "She is not with car."

"What do you mean?" said Eugenie, and then it dawned on her. "Oh, I see. Because I drove her home, she left her car here, and it's still here?"

"You got it," said Ralph. "At least according to the message she left while you were at the vet's."

"You didn't pick up?" said Eugenie, realizing from Ralph's expression that was the exact wrong thing to say.

"And she can't get a ride to the studio?" said Eugenie.

"According to the message," said Ralph. "Her...," he said, clearing his throat, "Partner is not available to drive her."

"Could you?" said Eugenie.

"No," said Ralph, without hesitation. "I'm the only one who knows about the paperwork."

"Paperwork?" said Eugenie.

"When I couldn't get into the system because I don't know the passwords," said Ralph, "I logged students in the old-fashioned way, using paper."

"Oh," said Eugenie. "Good thinking."

"Look," said Ralph. "Much as I don't like...," he started, then added, "If she's supposed to be here, then she better be here."

"I get it. I'm going," said Eugenie, tripping over the water and food bowls. "Would you mind moving or putting these away?"

Ralph shook his head. "Instructions from Martha are food and water bowls to be kept full and where Nandy would expect to find them."

Eugenie thought about that for a moment and a question occurred. Nandy might expect to find the food and water there, but if Eugenie couldn't even get into the studio because the security code kept changing, how could Nandy be expected to?

# 60

**EUGENIE WAS ALMOST** at Barbara's house when a barricade of emergency vehicles stopped her.

"What in the world?" said Eugenie. This was a modest neighborhood, but as far as Eugenie knew, a peaceful one.

A woman in uniform with a gun on her hip held up a hand, approached Eugenie's car, and motioned to let down the window.

"What's happening?" said Eugenie before the officer could get a word out.

"Everything's under control," said the officer. "But this is as far as you go."

"But I'm here to pick up a coworker," said Eugenie.

"The name," said the officer.

Eugenie gave Barbara's first and last name and then an awful thought occurred to her. Did all this have something to do with Barbara? Was Barbara okay? Was her partner?

"You know her address?" asked the officer.

"Hmm," said Eugenie, looking at a scrap of paper. "Here, I've written it down."

The officer read, then pointed across the street. "It's behind the line."

"I'm not sure what that means. Can I park? Can I walk over to the front door?" said Eugenie. "Is it even safe?"

The officer paused as a voice barked out something indecipherable from a communication device to which the officer answered, "Copy."

To Eugenie, the officer said, "Yeah, it's okay."

Eugenie was about to get out of the car when, across the way, she saw Barbara waving at her.

"That's her," said Eugenie to the officer. "That's the coworker."

"I'll have to check ID," said the officer, motioning to Barbara to stop in her tracks.

Barbara frowned but obeyed. With the officer looking on, Barbara lowered the large loose bag from her shoulder and rummaged through it, Eugenie assumed, in an attempt to find her driver's license. The search was not successful, and Barbara dumped the bag on the street. Though the officer's back was to Eugenie, from her body language, she appeared to be impatient to get back to something more important. Finally, Barbara pulled out not a wallet, but a single ID card. No wonder, thought Eugenie, she had such a hard time finding it.

The police officer looked at the house, Barbara, the ID, then said something into her collar.

Apparently, Barbara had passed because she headed toward Eugenie, in a pace typical of Barbara but one completely out of sync with all the surrounding activity.

Eugenie leaned over to open the passenger door. "My God," said Eugenie. "What's happening?"

"Oh," said Barbara. "Just neighbors who should never have married one another. This is the third time this month. I don't really care if they tear each other to shreds, but there's a dog my partner walks when they're at work."

"Geez," said Eugenie. "What the world needs is yoga."

## 61

**"ACTUALLY," SAID BARBARA,** after several minutes of silence passed between them in the car. "What the world needs is cheeseburgers. You know that place across from the studio?"

"I may have stopped there. Once or twice," said Eugenie.

"Thought so," said Barbara, giving Eugenie's middle a glance. "I didn't get a chance to eat. All the hoopla."

Eugenie decided to ignore the look, and the next voice they heard came from the fast-food speaker: "Welcome! What can I get for you today?"

Shit, thought Eugenie. It's Quincy.

"Hi," said Eugenie, hoping that by keeping it brief, he wouldn't recognize her voice.

But no luck.

"Well, hi," said Quincy. "I remember your order, and today I even remembered a boss tip. Communication isn't one thing; it's everything. Drive forward. Your order will be up before you can say, 'This ain't your daddy's burger joint.'"

"Think to ask what I might want?" said Barbara as Eugenie took the bags from the person at the window.

"Pretty sure there'll be a cheeseburger in there somewhere," said Eugenie. "If not two."

"If not three," said Barbara, extracting food out of the bags.

Eugenie laughed nervously. "Three! I'm not sure how he got that idea."

"We all have our demons," said Barbara, sinking her teeth into a bun.

Eugenie would have loved to ask what Barbara's were, but it didn't seem the right time. Instead, she said, "We got to get along. You, me, Ralph, somehow, we got to."

Barbara didn't hesitate. "You have this same conversation with him?"

"Sort of, but I'm not sure he really understood what I was trying to say," said Eugenie.

"When he gets the message, loud and clear mind you, then we'll see about this getting-along business," said Barbara. "Not before."

The cheeseburger in Eugenie's mouth went down her esophagus in one hard lump. She looked out the window. Across the way, the yoga studio sign blinked, noticeable even in the sunlight. Someone had forgotten to turn it off for the day.

Slowly she realized that someone was probably her.

# 62

**BARBARA WAS OUT** the door before Eugenie's car came to a stop. Now that's what a manager likes to see, thought Eugenie: enthusiasm.

But by the time Eugenie had parked and entered the studio, it was clear what was happening was anything but good. Ralph and Barbara were at it like two-year-olds.

Eugenie started to say something, gave it a second thought, then ducked into the library, closing the door with what she hoped was a meaningful slam.

This was never going to work. Not her being a manager, not Barbara and Ralph getting along, maybe not ever seeing Nandy again.

The thought made her sick to her stomach and she could feel the cheeseburger back pedaling up her throat.

Swallowing hard, she surveyed the small room. The works of sages and philosophers lined the walls. It was mind blowing to think of what they had gone through to achieve wisdom.

Compared to war and famine and chaos, what did one little lost dog matter?

She sunk into the lone chair with such weight that a few books fell off the shelf, one sending the suggestion box onto her lap.

Eugenie picked the box up, and the bottom flap, usually held fast by a metal clip, came loose and out fell a barrage of notes. Clearly, at this studio, there was no dearth of suggestions.

Eugenie sighed. There were dozens. So, this was to be her work for the day. Better than dealing with Ralph and Barbara.

Or, she started reading the notes, maybe not.

Classes are too expensive, said one. When had anyone said anything else? The next note said bathrooms could be cleaner. With that one, she had to agree.

But it was the third note that stood out. Not handwritten like the others but created on a printer, the type was small but readable, with a slightly threatening tinge to the font shape, making it seem more at home on a horror movie poster than in a yoga studio.

"We know you did it," the note started.

Eugenie dropped the note as if it were on fire, then remembering it was only paper, she scooped it up from the floor.

This time she read the entire message, focusing carefully on each word.

"We know you did it," it said.

"And, EP, if you think you'll get away with it, you're very wrong."

# 63

**FIRST, THERE WAS** knocking on the library door, then a voice. It was Barbara's.

"Manager of the studio. Oh, Ms. Manager."

Eugenie considered not answering.

Then she considered hiding.

But the chair was too small to hide behind, so she opened the door.

"Phone call for the manager," said Barbara. "And, Eugenie, since Martha's disappeared, tag, you're it."

"Who is it?" said Eugenie, upset that she was being asked to get out of the chair.

"Name wasn't given, and I didn't ask," said Barbara. "A man's high voice or maybe a woman's low voice."

"Right," said Eugenie, grabbing the desk phone. "Hello?"

On the other end, there was breathing.

"Hello?" said Eugenie again. "This is the, ah, the person you, ah, asked for."

The breathing continued, now louder.

"Hello?" said Eugenie, trying to contain her impatience. She reminded herself that she had, after all, been appointed manager and maybe this was something important. To bide the time, she raised one leg in tree pose.

On the phone, the sound of breathing stopped, followed by an abrupt "wrong number." Whether said by a man or a woman, it was hard to tell. Eugenie put the receiver down in the cradle so hard, she fell out of the pose.

She retreated to the library and started separating the notes, laying them out side-by-side on the floor. She categorized them as she went.

They fell into several groups: the air conditioning, the bathrooms, class prices, website issues, front desk issues, and teacher issues. There was even one that recommended wine be provided after every class. But the EP note, she now found to her dismay, was gone.

But where? She hadn't left the studio since the time she read it. Wait, she had gone to the desk to answer the phone. Had she dropped it there?

She went out to the front desk and found not Barbara or Ralph but someone looking lost and decidedly peeved.

## 64

**"WELL, HELLO," SAID** Eugenie, looking not at the visitor but around the studio for any trace of Ralph or Barbara.

"The sign by the door says you're open," said the woman.

"We are, sort of," said Eugenie, not remembering exactly what the studio hours were.

"I would expect someone at the desk if you are," said the woman.

Me too, thought Eugenie. Aloud, she said, "Just stepped away probably."

"Not good," said the woman.

Eugenie examined her. The woman was dressed in yoga clothes and not cheap ones. She looked ready for class, but there wasn't one scheduled for hours.

"What is it I can do for you?" said Eugenie.

"Martha said for me to come," said the woman.

Oh great, thought Eugenie, pausing then saying, "Uh, well, she's not here."

"I have her email printed out," said the woman.

Eugenie took a few minutes to read, wondering all the time where in the hell were Ralph and Barbara.

"I see," said Eugenie. "I'm afraid I know nothing about it, and well, Martha isn't here."

"So you said," said the woman, pulling the band out of her long thick hair and redoing the ponytail.

"Hold on," said Eugenie, "I may know someone who can help. Stay here. I won't be a minute." Which was not the first lie she'd told today.

Eugenie left the woman's side and scoured each room in the studio. As she passed the back door, she heard voices. She started to turn the knob, then hesitated. It was Barbara talking.

"Quick," Barbara said. "We haven't much time."

Another voice, Ralph's, Eugenie was sure, said, "There was Elle Pollo. Her classes were so popular she left the studio to start her own. Then there was Edward Peterson who faked his resume and when Martha found out, he was fired."

Eugenie listened carefully as Ralph's voice grew louder, as if to score a point.

"Then we get to the present time," he said. "The present time where there is only one EP at the studio, and that would be..."

# 65

**IT TOOK A** second to sink in. Eugenie had dropped the note somewhere in the lobby and one of them had picked it up and read. She didn't know what to do, only that she must think. Eugenie knocked hard on the inside of the back door, then dashed to the front door and opened it, saying to the startled visitor as she passed by, "They'll be with you in a minute."

Breathing hard, Eugenie managed to cross the outdoor walkway by circumventing the potted plant, but the steps to the red bus straight in front of her she didn't manage to avoid.

The stairs gave her something to stomp on and she did, with all her might.

The door at the top of the steps opened and a face that was in the habit of saying welcome, did just that.

"Please wait here," said the woman, pointing to a circle on the floor which read, if Eugenie hadn't gotten the message, "Please wait here."

Eugenie looked around and wondered what in the world she had gotten herself into. There were rows of beds on the right and left of the aisle, their ends raised to 45 degrees. Some kind of sticky mesh was taped to all the windows, and this gave her comfort she hadn't been seen entering the bus like a blind idiot. There was almost as much light inside as there was outside in the sun. She turned around to go out the door she came in, but a sign saying exit with an arrow pointing in the other direction stopped her. The arrow led to a second door at the front of the bus to the right of where a driver might sit if the seat hadn't been loaded to the ceiling with supplies. She was close to reaching the stairs out when a voice called her name.

It was Xavier without his white lab jacket on, and she'd passed him lying on one of the beds without knowing it. Shit.

"They'll be with you in a moment, really," he said. "They're efficient and I should know. I'm a gallon donor. Several, actually."

"Of what?" she wanted to ask. Then she noticed the tube hanging from his arm, and it all became clear.

"Oh, my goodness, of blood!" she said. "You're giving blood?"

"I guessed you'd be the kind of person who'd be here," he said.

Groan. Nailed. Now she couldn't leave.

All cheerful like he didn't have a needle sticking out of his arm, Xavier said, "In your business, you're always dressed to give blood, what with the bare arms and the comfortable clothes. Me, I have to change shirts." He motioned to his t-shirt with a complicated and undecipherable graphic on the front.

Feeling slightly sick, she didn't know what to say. A uniformed tech appeared at her side and said, "We're ready for you."

"See," said Xavier. "What'd I tell you? By the way, what's your type?"

She thought, well, he was. Not that it was any of his business.

The tech saw her confusion and said, "Newbie? Well, we're glad you're here. After we type your blood, you'll be able to tell him, not that you have to. It's your choice."

But was it her choice? Was any of this? A vision of Barbara and Ralph, heads locked together like conspirators, stuck in her mind. If she stayed put, at least it would give her time to think.

So, when the tech handed her a clipboard and said, "Just fill out the top little squares. It's asking for your last name," Eugenie felt she had no choice but to print out the letters - P.A.T.E.

# 66

**MINUTES LATER, HER** blood running out the thin long tube, Eugenie listened with half an ear to a second tech who had not stopped talking.

"If you want things to go faster, just keep squeezing the ball in your hand and think of all the lives you could be saving," the tech said. "A car accident every hour around here."

That, thought Eugenie, was no exaggeration. Her parents had been in one not a year ago.

A thousand times since she'd gotten herself into this bus, Eugenie thought about giving some excuse and asking to leave. Two things stood in her way. Apparently, her blood type could be used by the most people, not that she really understood why. But more significantly, at least to Eugenie, was the possibility that Xavier would see her leave the bus and know she had not been there long enough to donate.

She tried to let the "coach lounge," not "bed" as she had been corrected by the tech, take the weight of her head, but a poster of a lion tacked to the ceiling distracted her. Was the lion supposed to be comforting to those giving blood? What possible purpose could the poster serve? Was she supposed to be feeling brave as a lion by giving blood?

Well, she didn't. She felt like a fool and a coward. A fool because she wasn't paying attention and got into the bus in the first place. And a coward because the pinch of a needle was easier to take than being honest with Xavier or facing Barbara and Ralph.

Still, the donation had given her time to think and when the tech bandaged her arm, then gave her a cookie as a reward, Eugenie felt a smidge more capable of taking on Barbara and Ralph.

## 67

**THEIR REACTION WAS** not one Eugenie could have expected.

Barbara gasped when she saw the pink tape wrapped around Eugenie's arm.

"Not only a dognapper, but a vampire to boot," she said before Eugenie could get out a word.

Ralph, never one to miss correcting Barbara, sprung from his office computer. "Napper maybe, vamp, a definite no. They drink blood, they don't give."

"Have you both lost your minds?" said Eugenie, not giving into the f-bomb on her lips because a manager had to try and stay professional. "I donated because, well, it's a good thing and we should all do it."

"When pigs fly," said Barbara and Ralph in unison. Then they howled as if each had thought of it first.

"Where's the visitor who was here?" said Eugenie.

"There was someone here?" said Barbara.

"Yeah," said Ralph to Barbara. "Needed a high-level approach, so I sent you off to disinfect mats."

Well, thought Eugenie, that was something at least. Sweat and snot be damned.

"What did she want, this visitor?" said Eugenie.

Ralph smiled in recollection for several seconds, then pinned by Eugenie's stare, he finally spoke up.

"From the online teaching world," he said. "Something like a thousand followers, one of them a troll who graduated to scary stalker. Not hard to imagine, her looking like that."

Eugenie glared at Ralph, considered for a moment lecturing him on the politics of appearance, then decided that would have no effect.

"So, Martha offered her a job," he said. "A safe place. That's Martha, savior to the uninitiated."

"Where is she now, this visitor?" said Eugenie.

"Library," said Ralph, "Where all Martha's brainy notions go to die."

"Geez," said Eugenie. "All this time! Why didn't someone tell me?"

"Didn't occur in a million years that you might be giving blood," said Barbara. "Or should we say, doing penance?"

Eugenie shook her head and said, "You two. A few things we need to get straight. Later."

Barbara, not one to be intimidated by a person who had less blood than she ought, said, "Only a few?"

## 68

**EUGENIE FOUND THE** visitor sitting cross-legged in the library. She didn't even need a pillow to have her thighs meet the floor. The woman was like the models found on the cover of yoga journals which promised the possibility of not being able to pinch an inch, not anywhere on the whole body. Which Eugenie knew wasn't true, because, well, look at her.

The woman stuck out her hand. "Eesha Pandit. My Sanskrit name, not my legal one. I'll provide the necessaries when we've gotten that far. Have we gotten that far?"

"You mean hiring you? The front desk told me a little," said Eugenie.

"If it makes you feel any better, wherever I've taught, the desk was never any different," said Eesha.

Eugenie stifled a laugh and immediately liked this beauty a little better.

"Well, just so you know, they say I'm an interim manager, temporary, only until Martha gets back," said Eugenie.

"Poor you," said Eesha. "Big shoes to fill. That Martha's a powerhouse."

Not wanting to discuss Martha any more than was necessary, Eugenie asked if Eesha would share her work background, which Eesha did without referring to the resume she held in her hand.

"I don't recognize the studio names, but then they're miles away," said Eugenie.

"Would have to be. You don't start a new life in the same ballpark," said Eesha.

"I guess not," said Eugenie. "I'm sorry about what happened. Ralph told me."

"People can be shit," said Eesha. "Ralph, too, if you want my opinion."

Eugenie suppressed a smile. "Nothing to be done. He comes with the place. Martha's husband."

"You're kidding," said Eesha. "And I thought she was smarter than that."

Again, not wanting to go down that particular road, Eugenie said, "A teacher recently left and with Martha also gone, we've been filling with subs, but that's not a permanent solution. You teach Ashtanga?"

"Ashtanga, Nidra, flow, restorative, fascia release, you name it. Even have my own set of bowls if you're into sound healing," said Eesha.

"Not yet, but if ever a place could use it, it's this place," said Eugenie. "You heard about Martha's dog?"

"In a voice message. There was lots of weeping," said Eesha.

Eugenie looked off in the distance and said a silent prayer for the terrier. "Nandy's been gone several days now."

Eesha said nothing, but her large brown eyes, startling even without makeup, showed concern.

"Enough about that," said Eugenie, "Can you start tomorrow? Barbara will get you on-boarded and share the schedule."

Eesha reached out her hand and Eugenie shook it. The woman *was* beautiful, not that that was any excuse for stalking.

"Just promise," said Eesha. "There will never be any photos of me on the website."

"For obvious reasons," said Eugenie, wanting to show Eesha she got it. Still, it was a shame. No doubt about it, that face and body could bring in business.

# 69

**NOW THAT DECIDING** to hire Eesha was done, the only thing occupying Eugenie's mind was "cheeseburger."

Quincy's voice, dependable and confident, came out of the drive-through speaker.

"How may I help?" he said.

"A cheeseburger will do it," said Eugenie.

"Well, Eugenie, my sista," said Quincy. "You sure that's all you'll be needing?"

"That and a little advice if you got the time," said Eugenie.

"For you, anything," said Quincy.

A second went by, then two, and Eugenie realized the ball was in her court.

"A general tip will do the trick, nothing specific," said Eugenie.

"Mmm," said Quincy. "Let me see. Okay, got it. For a manager, the hot issue at the beginning of shift may not be the hot issue at the middle of shift."

"So, I take it this morning's issue's been resolved?" said Eugenie.

"I wish," said Quincy. "No, what I mean is this. The early issue hasn't been in any way, shape, or form solved. Instead, it's been struck through, obliterated, zeroed out, by another way-more-pressing issue. And the manager, well, the manager just has to deal. No patting yourself on the back before it's time. Know what I'm saying?"

"Thanks," said Eugenie. "Got to run. Cheeseburger's been delivered, nice and hot."

Eugenie, two bites into the burger, drove away hoping that the cheeseburger was the only thing that was hot.

# 70

THE STUDIO WAS quiet on her return and too soon, Eugenie assumed all was well. On her way to the bathroom to wash her hands of cheeseburger, Eugenie found Barbara, her ear to the door of one of the classrooms.

"Never let it be said I don't have your back," said Barbara in a whisper.

"What could you be doing?" said Eugenie.

"She says all the right things," said Barbara. "You know, the 'this is your practice, no one else's' and 'leave your comparing mind at the door' and 'just breathe' and hell, I forget what else."

"Who?" said Eugenie.

"Eesha, of course," said Barbara.

"Eesha?" said Eugenie. "She was supposed to start tomorrow."

"The usual teacher, I can't remember how to pronounce her name," said Barbara. "She called in sick at the last moment and well, Eesha was dressed and raring to go, so I let her rare."

Against her better judgment, Eugenie joined Barbara listening at the door.

"She has a nice voice, doesn't she?" said Eugenie.

"Perfect for chilling," said Barbara. "Oh, and you're bleeding."

"What?" said Eugenie, glancing down at the same time it occurred to her, it had been hours since she'd changed tampons.

"Made you look!" said Barbara. "No, not there. Your arm. The site of your one-pint-less."

Too late, they realized how loud they were being. With a confidence that had been evident since she showed up, Eesha poked her head out the door and said they were welcome to join her class anytime. And then the door was shut and this time tight.

"See what I mean about the woman?" said Barbara, rubbing her nose which had been hit by the door. "Chill to the bone."

**NO POINT SLEEPING** while Sarah was on a rampage. Eugenie had learned that long ago. She tried to ignore the pulses out of pure spite, but that had gotten her nowhere. Finally, Eugenie pushed aside the mass of curls wrapped around her face and squinted at her phone.

"It's like minus a.m.," texted Eugenie without reading anything but Sarah's name.

"I've been bumped," returned Sarah. "How could you?"

This was followed by a series of unhappy faces and a ridiculous amount of exclamation points.

"?????" texted Eugenie.

"Don't give me that. You hired her," was the response.

"Who? I cant do this Srh, it's nothing oclock. r U kiding me?" texted Eugenie.

Taking the number of errors to mean Eugenie's fingers weren't up to typing before the sun rose, Sarah called.

"Look," said Sarah, her voice soft with remorse, "I'm sorry for all the fuss."

Great. Now that Sarah was sorry, Eugenie was wide awake.

"What?" said Eugenie.

"It's just that she's so beautiful," said Sarah. "And accomplished."

"Who?" said Eugenie.

"The new teacher, of course," said Sarah.

"Technically, I didn't hire her. Martha did," said Eugenie.

"You mean mysterious Martha?" said Sarah. "The Martha who's disappeared along with her dog?"

"Grief," said Eugenie. "Everyone grieves differently. Maybe Martha does it by going into hiding?"

"When she's got a business to run?" said Sarah.

"Well," said Eugenie. "She did put me in charge."

"I know," said Sarah. "Go figure."

Eugenie took in a deep breath and said, "Don't you have something to do? I don't know. Shave your pits? Iron your tights?"

"Really?" said Sarah. "I should be ironing my tights?"

"It was a joke," said Eugenie.

"Oh, funny, ha ha," said Sarah. "Just wanted you to know how I feel. I mean years ago, I even took her online classes, you know, to grow as a teacher, and shit, she's good."

"If it makes you feel any better," said Eugenie. "No one will ever replace you, Sarah."

"Yeah," said Sarah with a laugh. "That's what Jared says."

## 72

**SO, THOUGHT EUGENIE** as she turned off her cell, they were back together. Sarah and Jared. Talk about things not making sense.

In a no-pain, no-gain mood, Eugenie ripped off the bandage from her arm. She noticed the puncture site had stopped bleeding and thought, well, at least there, something that was supposed to happen had happened.

And as promised by the tech, Eugenie had done good by donating. In the rest of her life, good was not so easy to do.

For one, she was thrown, more than she wanted to admit, by the fact that Sarah and Jared were back together but couldn't understand why. For as many aches and opinions as the guy had, Eugenie should be glad he was now Sarah's problem.

And yet, Eugenie was a certain age, not old but definitely not young, and could not help but allow a fleeting fantasy of living a life of luxury with a football player, even if he could no longer make any team's roster.

To change the subject, Eugenie decided to look around the house. The place came to her from her parents and in the months since they'd been gone, she'd done little, if any, organization.

She craved a cheeseburger and thought of Quincy.

What had he said? "Expect the expected. Or was it, expect the *un*expected?"

Eugenie couldn't deny the unexpected had happened in her life. Her parents had died in a car accident. Nandy was gone and along with the dog, Martha. Work had started on the back of the strip mall, but who had come up with the studio's portion and why? Eugenie had been asked to be manager and paid cash to do it. Eesha had showed up out of the blue.

The studio had been revealed to be a more chaotic place than she realized as a lowly teacher, and Eugenie yearned to go back to where she was only days ago.

She saw herself that fateful day eating a bear claw and watching teachers search for Nandy. It had been so easy because she had no responsibility and knew somewhere deep down that it made no sense to search for a dog who was no longer there.

Had Barbara and Ralph seen her lack of interest, and when they'd read the note accusing EP, figured that she was the culprit?

And if so, why hadn't they told Martha and why hadn't Martha asked her about it?

## 73

IT WASN'T MANY hours into the day, but despite this, cheeseburgers were on the grill and ready. Quincy's voice at the other end of the speaker sounded upbeat. Still, she was surprised when he offered advice without even being asked.

"The options are many," Quincy said, "But the path is narrow."

Eugenie laughed and said, "I love it."

"No, Sista," said Quincy. "I'm serious. Dead serious."

"Sorry," said Eugenie. "I wasn't laughing at you."

"Know you wouldn't," said Quincy. "Just that in this world, we're surrounded by wisdom and sometimes don't realize it."

"Okay," said Eugenie, not sure she was convinced.

"Watch for a sign," said Quincy, sounding a little too much like Eugenie's mother. "Know what I mean?"

"A sign? What kind of sign?" said Eugenie.

"Gotta go. Got. To. Go," said Quincy. Eugenie sighed then pulled over into a parking space and ate the cheeseburger, barely tasting it.

She looked at the stores and the employees walking into work, and she thought of Jared and wondered if he would show up to tap on her window.

And if that would be the sign.

After several minutes of seeing nothing out of the ordinary, Eugenie drove her car across the street to the studio strip mall.

There she parked in "Martha's spot" which gave her a boost of satisfaction she was amused to feel.

The day was blustery, and her loose hair whipped this way and that as she got out of the car. She scrambled in the glove compartment for a band to put her hair in a ponytail and as she looked through the windshield, she saw something on the grassy ground. It was as long as an alligator, but thank goodness, not the same color.

In the wind, it looked as if it might take flight and she ran to pin it to the ground.

Close-up, it was easy to identify: a feather flag like the one the studio had lost. On closer examination, Eugenie could swear it *was* the feather flag the studio had lost.

She picked it up and even though the wind tried to wrench it from her hands, she succeeded in bringing it all the way into the studio.

She thought of Quincy. And then her mother.

A sign indeed.

**NOT ONLY WERE** Barbara and Ralph, both hovering at the desk, unimpressed by the appearance of the flag, they were oblivious.

"Look," said Barbara, "If you took Nandy, just bring her back, and all's forgiven."

"How can you forgive Eugenie if it wasn't your dog that was taken?" said Ralph.

"'Cause I know Martha's mind, that's why," said Barbara.

"Really?" said Ralph. "Well, then you're the only one who does."

"I have my ways," said Barbara.

"Are they, by any chance, the same ways that cause you to faint?" said Ralph.

"Guys! Guys!" said Eugenie, "I need some help with the flag. Where to put it and strong arms to dig deep in the ground so it doesn't fly away again."

"Ralph can help," said Barbara. "I've got actual work to do."

"Sure, give the grunt work to the IT guy. That makes sense," said Ralph, picking up the flag and heading for the door.

As he passed Eugenie, he whispered, "Nice job kidnapping the dog."

# 75

**"I DID NOT** kidnap the dog," said Eugenie to Barbara.

"Fiver says you did," said Barbara.

"Why would you even think such a thing?" said Eugenie.

"A note that said EP did it, that's why," said Barbara.

"Anybody could have written that note," said Eugenie.

"You know about it?" said Barbara.

"Found when I opened the suggestion box in the library. I read it and must have dropped it somewhere, and you picked it up," said Eugenie.

"Yep," said Barbara. "And that's when things started to fall into place. How you weren't looking for Nandy that day when Fritzi said the dog was missing."

"Because I knew Nandy wasn't to be found in the studio," said Eugenie.

"Now," said Barbara, "That is suspicious. How'd you know that?"

"I can't explain," said Eugenie. "I just knew, that's all."

"Well, at least Nandy likes you," said Barbara. "That much was clear."

"I'm telling you," said Eugenie. "I didn't take the dog."

But Barbara was no longer listening. She had fainted once again.

# 76

**THE WOMAN WHO** answered the door looked so familiar, Eugenie forgot for a moment that she was holding onto a barely functioning Barbara.

"Fritzi?" Eugenie finally managed to get out. "It's Barbara, can you help?"

"Yikes," said Fritzi, who took one of Barbara's arms and steered both her and Eugenie to a bench on the porch.

"What happened?" said Fritzi.

"Okay," said Eugenie. "I'm confused. What are you doing here?"

"I live here," said Fritzi.

"With Barbara?" said Eugenie.

"Of course, with Barbara," said Fritzi. "Who else would I be living with?"

"She fainted," said Eugenie.

"I'm fine," said Barbara.

"No," said Eugenie. "You're not fine. Could you be pregnant?"

Barbara shook her head and Fritzi looked at Eugenie like she was crazy.

"I'm sorry," said Eugenie. "Am I missing something?"

"Just a little bit of something," said Fritzi, massaging Barbara's neck. "We live together, know what I mean?"

"Oh," said Eugenie. "I get it now."

"So, Babs couldn't be preggers, could she?" said Fritzi.

"Well," said Eugenie. "Something's up. This is the second time."

"She's fainted?" said Fritzi.

"Yes, and at the studio," said Eugenie. "And I've had to leave there to get her home. She said last time that someone would bring her to the doctor."

"It's not that far," said Fritzi.

"The doctor?" said Eugenie.

"No," said Fritzi. "The studio."

"Fritzi," said Eugenie. "The point is Barbara needs to see a doctor. I've got to get back. Ralph's been left running the place."

"Well now," said Fritzi. "That really is a problem."

 *77*

**THIS TIME EUGENIE** didn't have to pick up Barbara because she left her car in the parking lot. This time it was Fritzi who dropped Barbara off in front of the studio.

The minute Eugenie saw Fritzi pull in, she stopped clearing trash by the side of the building. As soon as Barbara was inside the studio, Eugenie rushed to Fritzi's car and knocked on the windshield.

She was met by many barks and a startled Fritzi.

"I need to talk to you," said Eugenie. "Do you have a minute?"

Fritzi parked in a space and tried to get out. Several dogs attached to leads beat her to it.

"You're still in business," said Eugenie.

"Yep," said Fritzi, "But only with people who pay and on time. Unlike you know who."

"Still holding a grudge?" said Eugenie.

"I wouldn't have stopped if I'd known you wanted to talk about her. Find someone else, why don't you," said Fritzi.

"Look, you're the one I need to talk to. I was just wondering if you told Barbara about your experience at the studio?" said Eugenie.

"Told her and told her and told her," said Fritzi. "But you see, before Barbara was hired, she was being treated by and I guess we're back to, whether I like it or not, you know who."

"Treated? For what, for heavens' sake?" said Eugenie.

"The fainting," said Fritzi. "Apparently certain crystals, you know, quartz and the like, are supposed to help."

Eugenie put her hand on Fritzi's car to steady herself, feeling like she too might faint.

"Please tell me Barbara has seen a doctor, been to urgent care at least," said Eugenie.

Fritzi nodded in an uncharacteristically solemn way. "Yep. Apparently, she's not supposed to get up too fast. Something with her blood pressure. She won't die from it, so not something that will affect her job."

"Fritzi," said Eugenie, taking a very long breath. "If you care about her at all, tell her to stay off the, ah, rocks, the crystals."

"Right," said Fritzi. "You try dealing with the zeal of the convert."

# 78

**BARBARA MIGHT HAVE** been a believer in alternative medicine, but two seconds with Ralph in the studio made it clear to Eugenie that he wasn't.

"I've updated the studio's liability release document," said Ralph. And to Eugenie's questioning face, he said, "You know the one that holds the studio harmless."

And to Barbara, he said, "Harmless no matter what. No matter where. No matter how. Harmless, harmless, harmless, get it? So, sign here."

"I guess," said Barbara, putting pen to paper and then stopping. "Wait a minute. Am I the only one who has to sign this?"

"Everyone has to," said Ralph.

"Prove it," said Barbara. "You two first."

After Ralph and Eugenie had signed and Barbara had read the entire document at a snail's pace, she finally signed.

"Studio's now safe," said Ralph. "From the effects of energy healing, insight cards, tea infusion balls, numerology, meridian tweaking, hypnotic suggestion, and bibliotherapy gone berserk."

"You know," said Barbara with a look that spoke so much trouble Eugenie jumped to move between her and Ralph. "You could use a little of that yourself, if you want my opinion."

"When I do," said Ralph. "I'll ask by talking into a can attached to a string pinned to a wall."

"Well," said Barbara to Eugenie. "And you said Ralph didn't have an open mind."

# 79

**THE MINUTE EUGENIE** stepped outside the studio, things improved. Getting away from those two was all she needed. She skirted the yellow ribbon by the side of the building and stomped on the underbrush, and by the time she got to the back, she felt herself again. No doubt the workers were almost done with the clearing needed to bring the strip mall up to code and she could cross that off her list.

But standing knee-deep in weeds, she discovered this was not the case. Down a few doors stood Xavier and before she had the chance to duck out of sight, he saw her.

"Yoo-hoo!" he called.

Something bit Eugenie on the ankle, and she swatted it with such force she almost toppled over. Xavier dashed to her side in time to steady her.

Instead of thanking him, Eugenie said, waving her hands to the sky, "Look, I can't understand it. The assessment was paid."

"Yeah," he said, pointing to the ruts left by the heavy equipment. "But you see what way those lead?"

"Back to the parking lot," Eugenie answered. "Unbelievable. And with the work barely started, much less done."

"This goes on much longer, I'm not going to have any staff," said Xavier.

"They're worried about fire?" said Eugenie.

"No," said Xavier. "They're pissed about having to take our patients out to the front parking where, due to precious little grass, there's squat to piss on, if you know what I mean. At least your clients and your teachers don't have that problem."

"Oh, don't worry," said Eugenie. "We have others."

"These businesses aren't a priority," said Xavier. "That's what the county website says, anyway. There's another project that's taking precedence."

On the other side of the retention pond, a thicket rustled from one end to the other.

Eugenie jumped and stifled a small yell.

"Probably a squirrel. Or a rabbit," said Xavier, and Eugenie thought, if so, that's one big bunny.

"You're not worried about bringing cats and dogs out the back when the work's through?" said Eugenie.

"Nah," said Xavier. "They're small and they're kept on leads. What's to hurt them?"

"Right," said Eugenie, drawing out the word with a long exhale.

"Look," said Xavier, "If you're not doing anything..."

Eugenie's mind was still on alligators, and it took her a moment to understand where this was going.

In the pause between his words and the resumption of her attention, entered a flying object, small and flat.

Xavier reacted but too late, and it hit him on the side of the head.

"Ouch," he said with no more force than if he'd whacked an elbow on the side of a chest of drawers.

It was left to Eugenie to show emotion. "What? What in the world was that?"

But Xavier could only laugh. "Not the only thing that's changed around here," he said. "You see that clearing beyond the far sago palms? Well, that is a frisbee golf course, put in a few days ago. And this...," he said, holding up the disc which had dropped to the ground by his feet.

"This is a shot gone a little wide."

# 80

**IT DIDN'T DAWN** on Eugenie until she was dressing for bed that Xavier might have been getting ready to ask her out before he got hit. The golf disc didn't seem to do him much damage, and she wondered if he would remember.

And if he did, what would she say if he asked her out?

Her first thought was that things were too complicated to get involved with anyone at the moment.

Her second thought was he was way slenderer than she was.

Her third thought was that he might have misgivings when he discovered how really ignorant she was about dogs and cats.

She fell asleep thinking not about Xavier, but about Jared and how nice things were when there'd been no strings. And before Sarah had re-entered the picture.

If it was dreaming of the tattoo on Jared's ankle as well as other parts north she expected, she was sorely disappointed.

When she did fall asleep, the vision that came to her was not Jared, but little Nandy. Nandy without a collar, Nandy, alone or with strangers, Nandy missing the home she'd had for so long.

Eugenie woke with a start. It was not guys she should be thinking of. It was dogs. And specifically, Nandy.

She dressed with a purpose. Her top and tights were, to her surprise when she looked in a mirror, matched and clean. She ate a bowl of oatmeal and didn't burn her lip once. On her phone, she searched for more tips on finding a lost dog. And feeling a confidence she hadn't felt in a long time, she knew what she would do.

## 81

**"RALPH," EUGENIE CALLED** out the minute she got to the studio. "Did Nandy have a chip implanted?"

Ralph stuck his head out the office door. "Like a potato chip?"

"Of course not," said Eugenie. "You know, one of those chip things that's implanted into pets."

"Oh those. Yeah. I mean no," said Ralph, "I mean, I have no idea."

"Ralph, this is important," said Eugenie. "We might be able to find her that way."

"Got me," said Ralph.

Barbara had entered the studio and was listening. "What's up?" she said.

"Apparently," said Eugenie. "Pets can be found if they've had chips implanted. Do you know anything about it?"

"From Fritzi, a little bit," said Barbara. "Did Nandy have one?"

"Ralph doesn't know," said Eugenie.

"No surprise there," said Barbara.

"Maybe we should just go on the assumption that Martha had one implanted in Nandy," said Eugenie. "Would that help?"

"Might," said Barbara. "But it's not like some GPS. You know, look at a screen and holy cow, discover that Nandy's in Tierra del Fuego."

"You'll need a shitload of sky miles," said Ralph, hunched over his computer. "That's a long way to go for a dog."

"Well," said Eugenie, ignoring him. "What does it do, this implant?"

"It has to be scanned," said Barbara. "At a vet's office or some kind of animal welfare place. If someone brings in a John Doe dog, the deal is to scan it for the microchip and that would give the owner's info."

"It's worth a shot," said Eugenie. "I mean, Nandy didn't have a collar on, that much we know."

"We do?" said Ralph, now on his feet next to the reception desk. "How?"

"I found it, the collar," said Eugenie. "When I was cleaning out the props closet the other day."

"Curiouser and curiouser," said Ralph.

"I didn't take the collar off and I didn't kidnap the dog," said Eugenie. "What I'm trying to do now is find the dog."

"Well," said Barbara. "If that's the case and we're all very interested to see if it really is the case, you're in luck. There's a vet a few doors down."

Not to be left out, Ralph scurried to the studio door and pointed. "Hasn't moved. It's still that-a-way."

# 82

IF SHE SHOWED up at Xavier's practice, it would look like she wanted a second opportunity to be asked out, and that was humiliating. If she didn't show up at Xavier's, Barbara and Ralph would know she had something to hide.

Eugenie decided Nandy was worth it and she soon found herself inside the office of Xavier Kip, veterinary to dogs and cats.

Only the vet wasn't there, as the tech behind the desk was quick to point out.

"Out judging a pet parade," said the tech.

"There's something as a pet parade?" said Eugenie.

"Around here?" said the tech. "Almost monthly. Owners got to get their money's worth out of those expensive costumes."

"And the pets like this?" said Eugenie.

"From their silence," said the tech, "That would be a yes."

The tech stood across from Eugenie and stared expectantly while Eugenie tried hard to remember why she was there.

"Well," said the tech, finally. "We're up to our haunches in flea powder. Can I get you some?"

"No," said Eugenie, now completely at a loss.

"Heartworm meds then?" said the tech.

"No," said Eugenie. "Not that. Ah, now I remember. Possible that you could help me find a lost dog who may have a microchip?"

"Easy enough to try," said the tech, looking toward a screen on the desk. "If the dog's been brought in somewhere else, it would show up on the database. Name?"

"Nandy," said Eugenie.

"Is that a first name or a last name?" said the tech.

"First," said Eugenie.

"And last?" said the tech.

Eugenie looked blank.

"Last name would be the name of the owner," said the tech.

"Oh," said Eugenie. "That would be Wetherell. Nandy Wetherell."

"Mmm," said the tech. "Not under the Ns and not under the Ws. Wait a minute. Isn't that the dog all the flyers around here mention?"

"The very one," said Eugenie, pointing. "The owner of the yoga studio down the way lost it."

"Hope it didn't end up in a dog fighting ring," said the tech.

"A dog fighting ring?" said Eugenie. "What is that?"

"You don't want to know," said the tech. "Beyond illegal, so buried deep, like Mariana Trench deep."

"Surely not...," said Eugenie, trying to remember Nandy's breed. "Not a ... terrier."

"Look, the less you know about this, the better," said the tech. "I'm doing my best to forget what I know."

# 83

**SADNESS OVERWHELMED EUGENIE** as she walked back to the studio. The thought of Nandy being forced to fight another dog - the little one wouldn't last a minute. It was too awful to think about, and a woman blocking Eugenie's way gave her an excuse not to.

"I'm your neighbor," said the woman.

Eugenie couldn't remember ever seeing her and dumbly said, "You are?"

"The title company next to your studio," said the woman.

"Well, not my studio. I'm just the for-the-moment manager," said Eugenie. "What? Is the music too loud?"

"No," said the woman. "Nothing like that."

Eugenie paused and waited, but the woman stayed silent.

"Look, I've got to get back," said Eugenie, motioning toward the studio door.

"I won't keep you, promise," said the woman, but again, she went silent.

"Would a class schedule help?" said Eugenie. "I'd be happy to get you one. We have some great teachers."

"I was hoping you'd be one of those," said the woman, her eyes filling with tears.

"I guess you'd have to ask my students," said Eugenie. "Look, you seem upset. Has the studio done something?"

The woman took in a deep breath. "My husband's threatened to leave me."

"Oh," said Eugenie. "I'm sorry to hear, but we're not, you know, I'm not a therapist."

"But you know exercises," said the woman.

"I don't follow," said Eugenie.

"If I don't get pregnant," said the woman. "He's threatened to leave me. I thought you could help."

"You see a specialist?" said Eugenie.

"More than you can count," said the woman. "I'm at my wit's end. I don't know what else to do. And I know it sounds crazy, but you are my last hope."

# 84

**CLUTCHING EUGENIE'S HAND,** the woman followed down the studio hallway to an empty classroom.

"I can show you some hip and pelvis openers. They might help," said Eugenie, although she doubted it.

"Anything," said the woman. "I'll take anything."

"Since you probably don't want to get down on the floor in those clothes," said Eugenie, "I'll demonstrate a few poses. Think you can remember?"

"No problem," said the woman. "My memory's not the issue. It's my ovaries and tubes that are."

"Okay," said Eugenie, sitting on the floor and putting her legs up the wall. "From this position, bring your legs into a V."

"Wow," said the woman. "I'm impressed."

"Don't be," said Eugenie. "I can't tell you how many of these I've done. The point is to stretch gently at first, then every day a little more. From here, you can bring the bottom of your feet together, like this."

"Think it will take more than a few months?" the woman said. "That's what he's given me."

"And lose the stress. Just relax. Breathe," said Eugenie. "It may sound stupid but try to think happy thoughts."

The woman's eyes narrowed.

"Sorry," said Eugenie. "Didn't mean that how it came out. My point is that with these poses, relax. Put pillows all around to support you. No strain. If music relaxes you, listen to that. Do you meditate?"

"Used to," said the woman. "But lately…"

"Time to get back on the cushion," said Eugenie.

"By the way," said the woman. "How far along are you?"

Eugenie wanted to scream. Instead, she took in a deep breath. Then, saved by the pinging of the woman's cell phone, Eugenie managed to smile.

The woman responded by saying, "Look, I got to get back. Thanks for your time. I'm like a really nerdy person and for me to do something like this is, well, out of character. Still, it was nice meeting you. When your growing family needs a bigger house, remember the title company next door."

## 85

BACK OUTSIDE, INSTEAD of patting herself for the good deed, Eugenie kicked a piece a trash down the walkway. It landed at the feet of a wildly gesticulating Sarah.

"The dog," said Sarah. "It's at the airport. I just heard the news report. Quick! Get in the car."

Sarah opened the door on the passenger side and Eugenie got in, then got out.

"Wait," Eugenie said to Sarah. "I've got to tell the desk."

"Get back in here you!" said Sarah. "I've already told them."

Before Eugenie had buckled the seat belt, Sarah was on the way out the lot.

"Sarah!" said Eugenie. "Slow down. What's the rush?"

"I thought you cared," said Sarah.

"Of course, I care about Nandy," said Eugenie. "But if someone's found her, we'll have to trust they'll keep her safe until we get there."

"Nandy's sneaky," said Sarah. "She ran away before."

Eugenie turned toward Sarah. "Wait, we don't know that. We don't know that Nandy left of her own free will or if she was taken."

"She wasn't happy, that dog," said Sarah. "I mean, she was always going over to you, right?"

"Well, right," said Eugenie. "But wait. If you think that means she wasn't happy, why are we trying to get the dog back?"

"Because I'm the one who's not happy," said Sarah.

Eugenie was trying hard to follow, but between Sarah's unpredictable driving and the way her mind functioned, it wasn't easy.

After a moment, Sarah said, "Look, I just want things to go back to the way they were."

"You mean," said Eugenie. "Getting pastries instead of payment for mandatory classes called by Martha?"

Sarah sighed deeply, then said, "Yes. Even back to that. The way things are now, you of all people are in charge, the new teacher is taking half of my students, and Jared's getting way too serious."

"Wait," said Eugenie. "I thought you liked Jared's attention."

"Things were better when he was with Martha," said Sarah.

"Jared was with Martha?" said Eugenie.

"All those private sessions," said Sarah. "Wake up, Eugenie. I mean, even Ralph knew, and he's not the brightest tool in the shed."

"No wonder he's been in a foul mood," said Eugenie. "Are you sure about wanting to dump Jared though, Sarah? I mean, he's loaded."

"If you're talking about his house and his car," said Sarah. "One belongs to his uncle and yesterday, the other was repossessed."

# 86

**AT THE AIRPORT,** the information desk knew nothing about a lost dog and recommended flagging down security.

Security was irritated to be asked about a lost dog when they were dealing with a worrisome, abandoned bag and they recommended, a little too eagerly, something unrepeatable.

Out of options, Sarah ran up to a shuttle driver who paused by the automatic walkway and said, "If there had been a dog lost here, where would it go?"

The driver pointed to a door past the bathrooms and said, "They might know. It's near the pet relief area."

Sarah pounded on a nondescript door and then ducked behind Eugenie just in time to avoid being elbowed by a very large, uniformed man.

"What?" growled the man who glared at them.

"We hear you have a dog, a lost dog," said Eugenie. "It was on the TV."

"Must be a real slow news day," said the man. "Name and breed?"

"Nandy's the name and the breed is terrier. Small," said Eugenie, showing with her hands the approximate size. "And a sort of creamish, brownish, grayish."

"Not even close," said the man, slamming the door.

Eugenie shot daggers at Sarah, who only shrugged and said, "Well, we haven't made the trip for nothing. The airport has a great poke bowl restaurant."

**IF EUGENIE NEVER** had to eat edamame again, it would be too soon.

Her stomach still churning, she walked into the studio. At the desk stood a bunch of clients signing papers.

To Eugenie's raised eyebrows, Barbara whispered, "The hold harmless agreement. But that one over there, how to say this politely, has declined."

It was Vicky, and it only took Eugenie a step toward her to smell the alcohol.

"Vicky," said Eugenie, "What's say you and me go to the library and talk?"

"Can't," said Vicky, giggling. "I forgot to renew my card."

"Not the public library," said Eugenie. "The one here. Come. I'll show you."

Vicky followed more out of curiosity than obedience, and soon she and Eugenie were sitting on pillows across from each other.

"First of all," said Eugenie, "The agreement is just a formality. I want you to know that I don't...none of us wants you to get hurt."

"Then quit seeing Jared," said Vicky.

Not Jared again. The man was an albatross around the studio's neck.

"I'm not seeing Jared," said Eugenie.

"Pinky swear," said Vicky, extending a finger.

"Promise," said Eugenie, mirroring Vicky. "Now, please sign the liability agreement, and we'll talk about welcoming you into class."

Vicky nodded, then tried to rise, but threw up instead.

Eugenie noticed with a twinge of pleasure that the vomit hit the diet book Martha had recommended.

Good, thought Eugenie, another one-star review.

**88**

**SARAH AGREED TO** cover Eugenie's class while Eugenie cleaned up the library.

The vomit had traveled further than Eugenie thought. Bits of spray covered two pillows and the suggestion box. As it had the last time she picked it up, the box opened to spill contents all over the floor. Eugenie skimmed them without much interest until she saw one with a familiar font.

"The dog is alive, and I know who's got it," said the note.

"Well," said Eugenie out loud. "For fuck's sake, share!"

From the adjoining wall came a pounding knock and Eugenie figured it was Ralph in the office telling her to cool it.

A yoga studio, even one in the state this one was in, had to do what it could to uphold its reputation as a place of calm.

Eugenie, noxious sponge in hand, sunk into a chair. Were they all being played with? And if so, why?

# 89

**THE HOUSE WAS** silent when later that day she slipped the key in the lock. Silent, as if only dead people lived there.

Ridiculous, thought Eugenie.

Her parents' bodies, a year ago reduced to ash, were stored one next to the other in a wall many miles away with only a sprig of plastic freesias to distinguish them from the other cremains.

It was their stuff that was left behind. Enough to fill a storage container, she thought, perhaps two.

She slowly walked down a hallway lined with floor-to-ceiling books and boxes and wondered why Arabelle had ever wanted to live there. Her bedroom was the only ordered place in the house.

Eugenie thought of trying the door to see if it was locked, then decided once was enough. She wouldn't like it if Arabelle went through her things.

And then, staring at some boxes labeled "Two Gals Moving Co. - Our Backs Hurt So Yours Don't," it was as if lightning struck.

Eugenie reached into her bag and found her cell.

"Hello Fritzi?" she said into the phone.

Fritzi hacked a smoker's cough and said, "Eugenie. Wassup?"

"It's time," said Eugenie. "If you know anything about Nandy, come out with it. Now."

# 90

**THE NUMBER OF** people who held a grudge against Martha could be counted on at least two hands, that much Eugenie knew.

There was Ralph, the cuckolded husband, and maybe the husbands before him. There were the other shop owners at the strip mall who were angry that Martha's delay in paying the assessment had made it difficult, if not impossible, to use their back doors. Then there was the long line of desk help who'd been fired. And don't forget Jared, she reminded herself. His "private lessons" might bring up issues that could cause him to react and not in a good way. And what about all the complaints that the classes were overpriced? And finally, there was Vicky, who was usually so high, there was no telling what she might do.

But it was Fritzi who had, in no uncertain terms, told Eugenie she was angry Martha owed her money, and that was a motive.

And it was Fritzi who was taking care of Nandy the day the dog disappeared.

Eugenie shook her head. She hadn't had to coax or threaten Fritzi on the phone to get an answer.

"How could you?" Eugenie said when Fritzi confessed.

"For a little money which I have now got," said Fritzi.

"Where did you hide the dog?" said Eugenie.

"In my house, which is why I didn't let you in when you dropped Barbara off," said Fritzi.

"And didn't Barbara notice Nandy was there in the house all along?" said Eugenie.

"What Barbara notices or doesn't notice is something I've given up trying to figure out long ago. Bab's smart in some ways, witless in others. Anyway, there are always lots of dogs in the house. Me, sometimes even I lose track of who's who," said Fritzi.

"But Nandy's okay?" said Eugenie.

"Of course, Nandy's okay," said Fritzi. "Would I lie about a thing like that?"

"You might. After all, my guess is you were extorting money from Martha in return for Nandy," said Eugenie. "And, not only that, but you left notes in the studio suggestion box. One accusing me."

"I needed to buy time. Put more pressure on Martha, and hey, you seem like the forgiving type, EP," said Fritzi.

Eugenie screamed in frustration.

"Calm down, you'll burst your tights," said Fritzi. "Things are actually going very well. Money was transferred this morning."

"From where?" said Eugenie.

"How should I know from where," said Fritzi.

"You mean you don't know where Martha is?" said Eugenie.

"Far as I know, nobody knows where Martha is. She just took off when Nandy split," Fritzi said.

"Nandy didn't just split. She had help," said Eugenie.

"You got to believe that Nandy's fine, and the drop-off place has been arranged," said Fritzi. "Tomorrow, corner of..."

"Don't tell me. Don't tell me!" said Eugenie. "I don't want to know."

"Oh," said Fritzi. "You of all people have to know. You're going to go in my place."

## 91

**AN HOUR OF** arguing didn't change Fritzi's mind one iota, and Eugenie finally relented. After all, it was the dog that counted.

Driving to the appointed meeting place the next day, Eugenie wouldn't have been surprised to see the police. Instead, there was only Martha.

She did not look happy.

"You're not Fritzi. And where's the dog?" said Martha to Eugenie's empty hands.

"There's been a slight hitch. I'm sure you've seen the weather report," said Eugenie. "With the hurricane coming on fast, a category 3, maybe a 4..."

Martha put her hands on her hips and seemed to grow an inch.

Eugenie took a step back and said as fast as she could, "Nandy will show up later on and at the studio, and please, don't kill the messenger."

"I won't," said Martha. "You don't have to tell me you're not behind this. Nobody needs an ethics class less than you."

"About that," said Eugenie. "I haven't been completely straight with you."

"Out with it," said Martha.

"First of all, I do eat the occasional cheeseburger from time to time at that place across the street," said Eugenie.

"Occasional?" said Martha, taking in Eugenie's middle.

"Okay. I lied about that. More than occasional," said Eugenie.

"No kidding," said Martha.

"And then," continued Eugenie, taking in a deep breath. "I had a friend help me with the last question on the yoga teacher exam. It was about a Sanskrit term and the test was timed and my brain froze and, well, she helped me."

"What was the question?" said Martha.

"What does 'Sa Ta Na Ma' mean?" said Eugenie.

"And what does it mean?" said Martha.

"Truth is my ID," said Eugenie.

"Close enough," said Martha, crossing her arms. "What else?"

"Well," said Eugenie. "Me and Jared. We've, we've, you know, done..."

"The deed," said Martha. "You and half the Western world."

"And well, that's it," said Eugenie.

"Now that you've gotten everything off your chest," said Martha. "Can we please get the damn dog?"

# 92

**EUGENIE DROVE HER** car to the studio, with Martha following in hers. The sky in front of them was a wall of gray.

"Where's Sarah?" said Martha to a startled Barbara at the desk.

"Why Martha, you're back, it's so good...," said Barbara.

"No time," said Martha. "I need to see Sarah to get updated on the studio."

"Sarah?" said Barbara.

"Yes," said Martha. "The Sarah I put in charge of things while I was away."

Eugenie, standing behind Martha, considered ducking into a bathroom, but decided to speak up.

"It was me," said Eugenie. "It was me you put in charge of the studio, at least according to Jared."

"Shit," said Martha. "I always get you and Sarah mixed up."

"Well," said Martha, looking around. "It doesn't look like you completely wrecked the place."

"Things have been going pretty..., well, sort of...," said Eugenie.

"Later," said Martha. "I just got the alert on my watch. Hurricane warning's been issued."

"A warning?" said Barbara. "Not even a hurricane watch first?"

Martha shook her head. "Good thing I came back when I did. Never did a bunch of people look more dim."

## 93

**MARTHA YELLED AT** Ralph to call in every available teacher, and then she took off in her car to get sandbags.

Sarah was the first to arrive, and when she was asked by Eugenie to move the library books away from an outer wall, she said, "You know, in New York, the yoga teachers are forming a union, so they don't have to do stuff like this."

"What?" said Eugenie. "Save their livelihood?"

"You're so dramatic," said Sarah. "And when you're swimming in dough from your parents."

"Hardly swimming, and I would rather have them than their money," said Eugenie.

"Right," said Sarah, considering. "Which reminds me. Jared and I broke up."

"Sarah," said Eugenie, throwing floor pillows out into the hallway. "Save it for someone who cares."

"Jealous," said Sarah, drawing out the word. "I knew it."

"I am not jealous," said Eugenie, who, hearing a loud knocking at the studio door, found Xavier on the other side.

The rain had started, and he was soaked.

He ducked his head in the door and said, "I've done everything I could at my practice. Need any help?"

Behind him, Martha pulled up in her car, and opening the trunk, dumped two sandbags at his feet.

"The back," she said. "With the retention pond likely getting fuller and fuller, it's the most vulnerable place in the studio."

"Hi," said Xavier to Martha. "I'm..."

"Stuff it with the introduction," she said. "Ralph! Where are you? Stop sandbagging and help me with the sandbags like a good boy."

But Ralph was now nowhere to be found.

# 94

**WHILE THE POWER** was still on, Eugenie decided to drive across the street to get cheeseburgers. The group would need sustenance if they got stuck in the studio.

That's what she told herself, but the truth was, she was the one who craved a cheeseburger.

And then, when she was about to give the order, Eugenie realized what she really needed was to hear Quincy's voice.

"How many?" said the voice in the box.

"Can you do, I don't know, ten?" said Eugenie.

"Sure, more if you need them," said the voice. "It's been quiet, what with the storm and all. People busy getting their to-do lists checked off."

"Is Quincy there?" said Eugenie. "I really need to talk to him."

"Nah," said the voice. "He's been promoted. Left for greener pastures yesterday."

The news hit Eugenie hard. His voice was so calm and cheerful. And what he said helped.

"Wait," said the voice. "He left a message. I'll make sure you get it with the order."

"A message?" said Eugenie, who couldn't imagine what it was. She pulled up and put her window down.

"Do you mind?" screamed a voice. "I'm getting soaked. Windshield wipers off if you please."

"Oops, sorry," said Eugenie.

"Everything in one big bag," said the girl, wiping water off her face. "You don't have to count. I did, twice. And here's a sticky note from Quincy. Hope it makes sense to you, 'cause it makes zilch to me."

Eugenie took the note from the girl's hand and read.

"XXOO, Q."

# 95

**BY THE TIME** Eugenie reached the studio parking lot, she felt like crying.

Her mother had signed travel postcards to her with the same message. X for kiss and O for hug. She had never written anything about what she and Eugenie's dad were doing because she believed that would jinx the trip.

But there was no time for memories. It was raining even harder now, and Eugenie dashed from her car into the studio. There, she tripped on Nandy's food bowl.

"Thank goodness," said Eugenie. "Nandy's back.

"Not really," said someone behind her.

Eugenie turned to find Vicky looking damp and smelling of spirits.

"Vicky?" said Eugenie. "What're you doing here?"

"Somebody...," said Vicky, trying to steady herself against the clothes rack, "Put out a call on social asking for help, so here I am. Besides, court ordered that I take yoga even though everything's canceled today. Whatever. Barbara gave me these cards to keep busy."

Vicky held out a stack, and several fell to the floor. Eugenie scooped them up.

"Let's go to the library," said Eugenie.

"Nope," said Barbara from inside the office. "Everything to be moved away from the outside walls."

"Got it," said Eugenie. "Let's try the middle classroom.

When they were both inside, Eugenie helped Vicki to the floor.

"And what," asked Eugenie, "Did Barbara say you were supposed to do with the cards?"

"They're one big crap pile," said Vicky. "All this ways and that. Discover the whole fucking meaning of life by way of Tarot mixed with some vision cards, animal, clouds, whatever. She said, hey Vicky, pull your weight, why don't you make sense of them? Well, if I do, it'll be the first time. Anyways, I've only done the Tarot. Pick."

"Vicky? You're kidding me," said Eugenie.

"Sure to cut the stress, though I don't know what everyone's so worried about," said Vicky. "There's holy lands to the west 'posed to protect us and there's a statue of a nun in a cemetery across the tracks guaranteed to stop hurricanes."

"Right," said Eugenie, "Maybe just for now, we listen to weather reports, and hey, here's an idea, look outside."

"No windows that I can see," said Vicky, eyeing the room. "And I thought *I* was the majorly off one. And since you're going to be that way about it, pick a card."

Figuring it was easier to go along than argue, Eugenie bent over and showed Vicky the message side of the card she picked.

"Ooh... death. Not the sunshine and lollipops we were expecting. Pick again," said Vicky, reshuffling the cards.

Wanting to do nothing less, Eugenie bent down to pick a second card.

"Oh!" said Vicky, her hand letting go of the card as if it stung. "It can't be, can it? Death...again."

# 96

**THE DOOR TO** the classroom flew open. It was Martha, and she did not look pleased.

"What are all these people doing here, and what are you two doing playing cards?"

"Don't know about them, but I was recruited," said Vicky, "And there's no playing. What's happening's serious. We're letting the future speak itself, I'm just saying."

Martha paused, then shook her head in disbelief. "There's work to be done. Your name's Eugenie, right? You stay. And you," Martha said, pointing to Vicky, "You go."

Eugenie turned to Vicky and said, "Promise me you won't leave the studio. The storm's getting worse, and it isn't safe."

When Eugenie and Martha were alone in the hallway, Martha, looking at the crowd around the desk, said, "Even more people! Unbelievable."

"Well, two things," said Eugenie. "The windows are plate glass, and we have... cheeseburgers for those who've come to help."

Martha rolled her eyes. There was a loud knock at the front door. "What now?" said Martha.

It took the owner a minute to get through the crowd of teachers and clients clustered around the desk, waiting instructions. Ralph was still nowhere to be found, and Barbara looked lost.

Another loud knock at the door, and Martha tried to open it. But the wind had picked up, and the door wouldn't budge. Finally, Xavier added his weight to Martha's. The door opened, and in came Fritzi.

With Nandy in her arms.

A yelp of joy erupted from the crowd.

Nandy looked terrified at the reception and buried herself in Fritzi's armpit.

"Oh no," said Martha, taking Nandy from Fritzi's arms. "That's not happening."

And to Fritzi, Martha said, "Don't you dare leave until we've talked."

Fritzi, for once, appeared cooperative, and Barbara came around the desk to give her partner a pat on the back.

"Long as everyone's here," said Martha. "There's work to do with the storm only getting worse."

And, as if on cue, a heavy branch tore from a nearby oak tree and hit the studio door, making everyone jump.

# 97

**"GREAT," SAID MARTHA.** "The front door's blocked."

"Well," said Eugenie. "We do have cheeseburgers."

"Stop already with the cheeseburgers," said Martha. "Do we have water to drink and to flush toilets?"

"For the moment," said Barbara, and the words weren't out of her mouth before the power went off.

A dozen people groaned in response.

"Flashlights, two, maybe three, are in the utility closet," said Barbara. "Now! While there's still light from the outside."

The sound of wind grew louder, and all Eugenie could think of was that she had drawn the death card.

Twice.

Someone handed her part of a cheeseburger, and she ate it without tasting.

After the last swallow, Eugenie heard the roof groan and the sound of a tree snap.

"Quick," said Martha. "Everyone into the center classroom."

The roar of the storm, when the door was finally closed, lost some of its fierceness and Eugenie began to breathe a little more easily.

Then came another loud knock, followed by screaming.

Eugenie recognized Ralph's voice and followed Martha out of the classroom and into the hallway.

Ralph had squeezed behind the branch blocking the front door and was yelling, "Let me in!" at the top of his lungs.

Martha shook her head and motioned to the side of the building.

And if that wasn't clear enough, Eugenie screamed, "Back door!"

For a moment, it seemed as if Ralph couldn't hear them. Then he nodded, and they watched as he darted toward the side of the building.

Martha turned and yelled, "Whoever is near the back door, open it now!"

Unfortunately, that person turned out to be Vicky.

## 98

**"I GOT IT!** I got it!" said Vicky, releasing a squirming Nandy from her arms so she could open the back door.

As a sodden Ralph came in with bottled water enough for a week, Nandy, thinking this was the most fun she'd had in a long time, dashed out the door.

"Oh no!" screamed Eugenie, sprinting after the dog. "Nandy! No!"

Outside, the wind had lessened, and in the relative calm, she could see the little dog darting back and forth across the far bank of the retention pond.

"Nandy," said Eugenie, squatting on her heels and holding out her arms. "Nandy girl, come here."

The crowd from the desk squeezed behind Eugenie and, recognizing what was at stake, held their tongues.

Something about the sight of all these people made Nandy stop and cock her head in curiosity.

Slowly, Eugenie made her way until she was within a few feet of the dog. "It's all right, Nandy. You're okay," she repeated in soothing tones.

And just like that, the dog walked into her arms.

Eugenie stood, almost lightheaded with relief, and it was then the wind started to pick up again.

As she rounded the edge of the retention pond, something let loose from a tree and flew in her direction.

Eugenie recognized it as an errant golf disc, and Nandy, thinking that, once again, this was a game, leaped into the air in an attempt to grab the flying object.

But the disc eluded the little dog, and first, one fell into the pond, followed by the other.

From the far end, audible above the wind and the flailing branches, came a loud, determined, and most ominous splash.

# 99

**"GATOR!" CRIED A** voice in the crowd, but Eugenie already knew what she was up against. After all, she and the creature had met. One early morning in the parking lot.

As her ears tried to block out the screams, Eugenie waited for someone in the crowd to move. To herself, she counted one Mississippi, two Mississippi... But when no one moved, it was then that Eugenie knew if someone was going to save Nandy, it would have to be her.

She kicked off her flip flops and dived, or rather belly-flopped, into the pond. It was more belly than flop, but it served to keep her eyes above the dark water. Frantically, she looked around for Nandy.

She knew that within local ponds lived a million hazards from weeds to discarded ottomans to, well, she didn't want to think about it. Only when she realized her flat dive had worked did she feel any hope.

There was the dog and less than a few strokes away. So close. Eugenie only had to use arms strengthened by hours and hours of yoga to reach Nandy.

And in the next second, she had. She scooped the dog up by the belly and looked for a way to propel it to safety.

Arms were outstretched in Eugenie's direction, and in her haste, she picked one, hoping it was the right one.

Whoever caught the dog backed out of sight, but the voices, instead of getting softer, only got louder.

"Get out!" said a male voice, whose she couldn't tell. "Now!"

Another arm reached toward her, but as she tried to climb the slippery bank of the pond, it was clear something held on fast to her leg.

# 100

**EUGENIE WIGGLED HER** ankle once, twice, then again, trying to figure out what was keeping her stuck in the pond. What is it? A weed? Algae? Or, oh no, not...

The screaming continued with even more arms reaching in her direction in what was now a futile attempt to pull her up on shore.

Vicky's screams, decibels above the others, told Eugenie she didn't have much time.

With as much force as she could muster, Eugenie yanked hard, and finally, the ankle came free.

In a shot, she was in someone's arms and being lifted over sandbags and dragged back toward the studio.

She heard the scuffle of feet and the door pound shut, and that was all she heard.

For the world had turned very, very black.

## 101

**SHE WOKE TO** Arabelle and Xavier hunched over her.

"Arabelle," said Eugenie. "Wait, Arabelle? What are you doing here?"

"Never mind," said Arabelle. "We just need to check you out."

"And Xavier?" said Eugenie.

"I'm here," said Xavier. "I'm here."

"He may be here, but from what I understand, he's a vet," said Arabelle. "Maybe he could attend to the dog while I, being trained in first aid for humans, could be left, I don't know, to attend to you."

"Nandy?" said Eugenie.

"She's okay," said Xavier. "She appears to be okay. Now take it easy and let us take care of you."

"Ouch," said Eugenie. "That hurts."

"Your ankle," said Arabelle. "Something sharp broke the skin. With all the junk in that pond, your tetanus up to date?"

"I think so," said Eugenie. "Vaccine lasts for years."

"Right-O. Brain seems okay," Arabelle said to Eugenie. "And Barbara, that your name?" said Arabelle, looking off to the side. "Could you get the damn rocks, the crystals, the whatever, you've laid all over the place out of here?"

With Arabelle distracted, Xavier entered Eugenie's field of vision for a second time. "What's your first and last name, and where are you?" he said.

Eugenie smiled and said, "Eugenie Pate and I'm in the most exciting yoga studio around."

"You could say that again," said Arabelle. "Rest now. Your ankle's wrapped and...," she said, looking up at the group, "If anyone opens a door before I give the okay, make no mistake, I'll make sure that's the last thing they ever do."

# 102

**NOT LONG AFTER** the cheeseburgers disappeared and before all the bottled water had been used to flush toilets and hydrate the group, the storm was over.

Eugenie still lay on the floor, supported by assorted mats and Indian blankets. A small pillow had been placed over her eyes against the shock of the lights coming back on.

Arabelle gently took it off and asked Eugenie how she was.

"I'm okay," said Eugenie.

"Let's make sure you can walk on it," said Arabelle. "Before I have to leave."

"What is it you do again?" said Eugenie, slowly getting up. "You're awfully good at this nurse stuff."

"Far from it," said Arabelle. "We'll talk at home. Right now, you're looking better than anyone ought to, and I got to go."

Eugenie nodded and limped to the bathroom.

She flushed a toilet just to make sure it worked, then gratefully sat down.

From the stalls around her came muffled voices.

"Did you see that?" said one.

"If I live a million years...," said another.

"That's one lucky dog," said a third.

## 103

AT HOME, EUGENIE slept, took some aspirin, then slept again. When she finally got up, she was surprised to see Arabelle in the kitchen. And she was even more surprised to see Arabelle's bags packed and ready to go.

"My work here is done," said Arabelle to Eugenie's raised eyebrows.

"So, if not a nurse, what is it that you do?" said Eugenie.

"Private investigator," said Arabelle.

"Very private, I would say," said Eugenie.

"I didn't know what you knew or didn't know," said Arabelle.

"About what, for heaven's sake," said Eugenie who, feeling her ankle ache, sunk into a chair.

"Well...," Arabelle started.

"Wait a minute. I bet I know," said Eugenie. "There was that photo of a man."

"Thought you had been in my room," said Arabelle.

"There was a noise I had to check out," said Eugenie.

"Oh, really?" said Arabelle.

"Yes, really, a clanking sound," said Eugenie. "Turns out it was one of those robot vacuum cleaner things, on auto-timer, I guess."

"Keep one with me always," said Arabelle, kicking a backpack about to tip over. "Still, it didn't make you look good, considering."

"Considering?" said Eugenie.

"Considering that I wondered if you were connected with the guy in the photo," said Arabelle.

"Well, if you must know," said Eugenie. "I'd seen the photo before. Security guard at the yoga studio parking lot showed it to me."

"And?" said Arabelle.

"No idea who the guy in the photo was. Is," said Eugenie.

"So, it seems...," said Arabelle, "The jerk was only after Lizbeth, Martha, and Eesha."

# 104

**"LET ME FIX** you some sweet tea," said Arabelle. "You look pale."

Eugenie had sunk even further into the chair and had no strength to disagree, even though the idea of tea didn't appeal.

"Martha's second husband," said Arabelle, handing Eugenie the mug. "Held a grudge against her, which spread to other yoga teachers and students. Martha was in denial for a long time, but it was Lizbeth's sudden departure that made her wonder."

"Oh no!" said Eugenie. "I knew Lizbeth. She was in some of my classes."

"Lizbeth's mother was outraged at what happened. And when the police came to a dead end, she hired me," said Arabelle.

"But wait," said Eugenie. "Eesha got caught up in this, too? She hasn't been here that long."

"Guy's an idiot with his rackety bike and twitchy fire-alarm-pulling fingers. Still, he was able to stalk her after she left other studios," said Arabelle. "And then put two and two together and figure the only place around here, Eesha, by the way, her real name is Carol, would be caught dead in was Martha's."

"How convenient for him. Get back at Martha at the same time he finds Eesha, I mean Carol," said Eugenie. "Geez, where is he now? Are they in danger?"

"Why I made it a point to go to the studio in the storm," said Arabelle. "As they say, in chaos, there's opportunity."

"The guy showed up there yesterday?" said Eugenie, a shiver running down her spine.

"He figured, rightly as it turned out, that Martha and Carol might be there," said Arabelle.

"Did you actually see him?" said Eugenie.

"No," said Arabelle. "But a camera outside the title company next door caught him fooling with Martha's tires."

"So," said Eugenie, eyes wide, looking out the window. "Where is he now?"

## 105

**"JAIL," SAID ARABELLE.** "Very much in. And that means I'm outta here. On to the next job. Might see you again when I have to give testimony. Might not. Anyway, keep on keeping on with those chaturangas."

"Alligator pose?" said Eugenie, shaking her head. "Might be a while before I'll be doing that again."

"I guess," said Arabelle, chuckling as she headed out the door. "Wow, what you did. Maybe it was all those cheeseburgers."

With Arabelle gone, Eugenie headed for the beach. After all, Martha had told her to take the time she needed. And the saltwater cure might be just the trick.

It being a weekday and the storm having wrecked much of the shoreline, there weren't many people. She laid out a towel on what was left of the sand and walked into the water. Her ankle stung for a minute, then went numb. That, Eugenie figured, was a good thing.

Feeling her spirits lift after a short swim, Eugenie walked the length of the narrow beach as it curved toward the causeway. She breathed in the fresh air. There was something about a storm passing that made things feel new again.

She thought of her father, who lived within miles of the shore but never visited, and her mother, who was so superstitious she wouldn't make a move without reading her horoscope. They had had their quirks, Eugenie realized, but then so did she.

Maybe it was time to go through her parents' things. Maybe it was time to make her home really her home.

# 106

**TO ARABELLE, CHAOS** might be opportunity, but to Eugenie, going through box after box of her parents' stuff, clutter was all it was.

That is until she opened a box labeled "photos."

Her father was the photographer, and there were a million pictures of Eugenie's mom, a few of him and none of her.

She was their child. Didn't parents take pictures of their child? Especially an only child.

As Eugenie grew angrier and angrier, her ankle began to throb, and she limped off to find aspirin.

Then, on the way back to the box, she found a photo that had escaped and lay propped on a table leg.

Eugenie picked it up and immediately recognized herself as a small girl, maybe four or five years old. She turned the photo over to see if there was a date, and she'd been right. Here was a photo of her at five.

And she was standing between two kneeling parents who cocked their heads in her direction and smiled widely.

# 107

**HOLDING THE PHOTO** in her hands, she sat on the couch her mother had stewed over for months and finally purchased.

If Eugenie ever needed a reminder that she was theirs and that they loved her, this photo was it.

The aspirin finally kicked in and, with it, a better frame of mind. She drove to the studio.

There, things seemed to be much the same. Barbara and Ralph were fighting at the front desk. Martha was straightening the yoga gear for sale. Students were coming out of Eesha's Ashtanga yoga class, looking soaked and impressed with themselves.

Eugenie stood still and took everything in. For a second in that muddy pond, she had wondered if she would ever see this place again.

But there she was, dressed and ready to teach.

The door behind her opened, and a uniformed man stuck his head in.

To Eugenie's startled face, he said, "Fish and Wildlife Conservation Commission officer. Just confirming the gator is in our possession." Then he nodded with satisfaction toward the truck in the parking lot and said, "And will be transmigrated."

Ralph piped up: "Will be what?"

"Translocated," said the officer.

"Huh?" said Ralph.

"Moved," said the officer, "Someplace else, not near humans. Even though we're near the end, mating season is what does it. Makes them ornery. Just like with people, lust cracks the brain."

To this, no one in the studio could think of a single thing to say.

"Well," said the officer, tipping a non-existent hat. "Just wanted you to know. We'll report to the department doing the work behind the building that they'll be able to start up again. Back doors will be an option and soon, now that things are safe."

Deep in thought, Martha placed a pair of tights on the rack in such a way that its hanger and the two next to it fell off. Something in Ralph's eyes softened as he watched his wife pick up the gear from the floor and smile at him.

Meeting her look, he said gently, "Not to worry. No matter what. That door will never be opened again."

## 108

**BY THE END** of the day, Eugenie had taught a class, received a raise, and had her photo taken with Nandy.

The class was filled with the usual model wannabees, but this time, Eugenie stood up front with a startling goodwill toward them and herself.

She let one student after another demonstrate their favorite asana. The students smiled when they discovered a shared interest and cheered when they discovered a fellow student could do something they never dreamed of doing.

There was so much happiness that at the end of class, the students didn't want to leave, and Eugenie had to go around picking up props so the next class could start on time.

The most beautiful student lingered after the room emptied, and Eugenie, remembering how the last class with this student went, asked if everything was okay.

"Could I hug you?" said the woman.

"Ah," said Eugenie, "I guess."

"I heard all about it. What you have, I need some of," said the woman. "And I thought hugging you, it might rub off."

"Happy to try," said Eugenie, still not sure if she was being set up.

And yet, the hug when it happened, was long and genuine.

When the woman finally pulled away, Eugenie was surprised to see tears in her eyes.

"You never know what you're made of until you're tested," said Eugenie, thinking that maybe a little of Quincy had rubbed off on her.

As the woman left the studio, Eugenie patted a pocket in her tights to see if the check Martha had given her earlier was still there.

It was, and she bent to locate her flip flops in a lower cubby.

Behind her, the studio door opened, and in flew a woman dressed in business casual.

"Sorry," said Eugenie, still trying to find her sandals. "The person at the desk stepped out. But they'll be back in a moment to help you."

"Oh," said the woman. "It's not them I want, but you."

Eugenie straightened, trying to put a name to the face.

"You remember. Of course, you must remember. The owner next door," said the woman. "Of the title company."

"Oh yes," said Eugenie. "The one who was trying to get..."

"Pregnant!" said the woman. "Well, I am!"

"So soon," said Eugenie. "Are you sure?"

"They say it happens all the time during hurricanes," said the woman. "Anyway, I don't need a test to tell me what my body knows. And who to thank."

And with this, she handed a framed photo to Eugenie.

Amazed, Eugenie took a look. It was the photo Martha had taken. There was the unmistakable wavy hair, the muffin top no yoga gear could hide, and finally, there was Nandy, looking in Eugenie's arms, the size of a coconut.

"Where did you get this?" said Eugenie.

"Off the studio's website," said the woman. "Haven't you seen? Did I peg you right or what? It says, and wow, this just gives me chills, 'Yogini Eugenie, Hero.'"

 **109**

**THE FRAME TUCKED** securely under her arm, Eugenie found Xavier waiting by her car.

"Hi," he said. "You okay?"

"Yes," said Eugenie. "Ankle's healing nicely. It wasn't that big a deal."

"From what I saw," said Xavier. "It was a very big deal. In fact, I've never seen anything like it."

"And all without health insurance," Eugenie said and laughed.

"Even more impressive," said Xavier. "Look, I just wanted to ask you..."

"Yes?" said Eugenie.

"I just wanted to ask you. Are you and Ralph a couple?" said Xavier.

Eugenie couldn't get the words out quick enough: "Whatever gave you that idea?"

"It's just that you ended up in his arms, on the side of the pond, you know, with the gator on your heels," said Xavier.

"Xavier, I would have hugged a sphinx at that point," said Eugenie.

"So, if I asked you out, you might say yes," said Xavier.

"To a pet parade?" said Eugenie.

"I was thinking something more like a concert," said Xavier.

Eugenie smiled and turned. With a wave, she said, "Call me!"

Then, remembering she'd left a book in the studio, she walked to the front door.

Running her fingers over the raised letters, slightly the worse for wear from being scarred by the windblown branch, she read, "Martha's Mat - Your Life will Change when You Get on Yours."

Smiling to herself, Eugenie opened the door. She promptly fell over Nandy's water bowl and this time, it was the best feeling in the world.

*The End*